D0327897

"Sign the divorce, Teo." Skye used

er

Clare Connelly was raised in small-town Australia among a family of avid readers. She spent much of her childhood up a tree, Harlequin book in hand. Clare is married to her own real-life hero, and they live in a bungalow near the sea with their two children. She is frequently found staring into space—a surefire sign she is in the world of her characters. She has a penchant for French food and ice-cold champagne, and Harlequin novels continue to be her favorite ever books. Writing for Harlequin Presents is a long-held dream. Clare can be contacted via clareconnelly.com or her Facebook page.

Books by Clare Connelly

Harlequin Presents

Bought for the Billionaire's Revenge
Innocent in the Billionaire's Bed
Her Wedding Night Surrender

Visit the Author Profile page
at Harlequin.com for more titles.

Clare Connelly

BOUND BY THE BILLIONAIRE'S VOWS

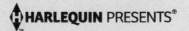

ISBN-13: 978-1-335-50460-9

Bound by the Billionaire's Vows

First North American publication 2018

Copyright © 2018 by Clare Connelly

This edition published by arrangement with Harlequin Books S.A.

Printed in U.S.A.

BOUND BY THE
BILLIONAIRE'S VOWS

For Arlene, who is courage, strength and resilience personified.

Not to mention, a very dear friend.

PROLOGUE

Six years earlier

'CAN YOU SEE IT, Matteo?'

The newspapers loved to say that Matteo Vin Santo didn't have a heart, but they were wrong.

Observing his grandfather lying weak and pale against the ordinary hospital bed-sheets was making that very organ clutch and grip painfully. The certainty that the man had only hours left to live was ripping it apart completely.

'See what, Nonno?'

'Nonno?' Alfonso Vin Santo smiled, but his lips were chapped and the pain turned the instinctive gesture into a wince. 'You haven't called me that in a long time.'

Matteo didn't respond. His eyes fell to his grandfather's hands. Hands that had shaped a corporate empire; hands that had been at the helm during its demise. He looked away, focusing on the uninspiring view of the outskirts of Florence.

'See the water? You always loved the way the sun bounced off it, no?'

Matteo's eyes swept shut. Though they were in a linoleum-floored hospital room, he pictured exactly what his grandfather was seeing. The view from the terrace of Il Grande Fortuna, the hotel they'd once owned in Rome, overlooking the Tiber in one direction and the Vatican in the other.

Anger—a familiar response when he thought of the hotel—churned his gut. It was fierce in that moment, so fierce it almost took his breath away.

'Yes. It's beautiful.'

'It is more than beautiful. It is perfect.' Alfonso sighed and then a ghost flickered across his face. A moment of clarity that brought with it pain. 'It was my fault.'

'No, Nonno.' Matteo didn't mention that bastard Johnson's name. There was no need to hurt his grandfather further at the end of his life. But *he* was the man who was to blame. He was the cause of Alfonso's sadness now—him and his stubborn refusal to sell the hotel back. A refusal he'd taken with him to the grave.

But Matteo could fix it.

He *would* fix it.

'I will get it back for you,' he said, and the words were spoken with such soft determination that it wasn't clear if Alfonso had even heard. It didn't matter, though.

The promise was one Matteo made to himself as much as the old man.

No matter what, no matter how, he would return the hotel to his family.

At any cost.

CHAPTER ONE

'DO YOU HAVE an appointment?'

An appointment? With her own husband? Skye clutched her handbag tighter, thinking of the divorce papers contained within the soft kid-leather. A hint of perspiration ran between her breasts and she shifted uncomfortably. Though the luxurious foyer was well air-conditioned, Skye had been sweltering since touching down at Marco Polo airport earlier that day. Travel weariness, and the exhaustion that had dogged her since walking out on her marriage to Matteo, combined to give her a sense of overwhelming desperation at the task ahead.

'Signor Vin Santo has a full afternoon. I'm sorry,' the receptionist murmured, her expression offering no corresponding apology. If anything, it was all manicured smugness.

Skye's voice was soft when she spoke, weakened by the difficulty of what lay ahead. Divorce was essential—and it had to be now. She'd go to almost any lengths to get Matteo to agree easily. She needed his signature on these papers so she could get the hell out of Italy. Before he discovered the truth. 'If you tell Matteo I'm here, I'm sure he'll cancel whatever he has on.'

The receptionist's disdain was barely concealed. '*Signorina…?*'

Skye's own smile reflected the other woman's emotion. It was a common mistake. Skye was only twenty-two and she was often told she looked younger still. The make-up she'd applied painstakingly that morning had sweated off throughout the day, and she stood in the impossibly glamorous offices feeling as out of place as she had been in their marriage. Nonetheless, she had a right to be there. A reason. She tilted her chin, staring down at the receptionist as though this weren't the culmination of all her nightmares.

'*Signora,*' Skye corrected emphatically. 'Signora Skye Vin Santo.'

Skye had the satisfaction of seeing the other woman's mouth form a perfect red 'o' of surprise, but she recovered swiftly, reaching for the telephone and lifting it to her ear. Her eyes dropped to Skye's finger and Skye was glad she'd slipped the ten-carat solitaire back into place for the day. '*Mi dispiace!* I'm so sorry, Mrs Vin Santo,' the receptionist said, pressing a button and waiting for the phone to connect. 'I had no idea Signor Vin Santo was married.'

Skye's nod was dismissive, but the words cut

deeply. Why should this woman have known of her boss's marital status? It wasn't as though they'd been married long. Skye had walked out on him after just over a month. A month too long.

How had she been so fooled by him even for that period of time? Hell, why had she even married him? That was easy. Out of nowhere, an unwelcome image of Matteo flooded her mind's eye, reminding her of how he'd been the evening they'd met. In a cocktail suit, so handsome and charming, so intent on seducing her. She'd been so easy to seduce and he'd been so persistent. Fate, she'd told herself at the time. Lies, she'd later discovered. All of it.

She heard the rapid-fire Italian conversation without comprehending. Her eyes were fixed to the view of Venice, a city she'd once adored with all of herself. A city she'd thought she'd spend the rest of her days in. She hardened her heart to its charms now, ignoring the way the gondolas glided past, full of grace and pride; the way the water formed glistening little sunlit peaks and troughs as it was stirred by the activity. She ignored the way the ancient buildings huddled together, singing the secrets of their souls, the way the bridges seemed to emote wisdom and strength. She ignored the dazzling colour of the sky and the birds she could see but not hear—she didn't need to hear them to remember the way they sounded. The flapping of their wings was the breath sound of Venice.

It was beautiful, but it was no longer for her. Skye spun round, glad to turn her back on the view, even when it meant she was staring at the disdainful receptionist once more. The woman stood—she was taller than Skye had been able to appreciate while seated—and made her way to stand directly in front of Skye.

'Signor Vin Santo will see you now. Is there something you would like? Some water? A soda?'

Vodka, Skye thought with a wry smile. 'Mineral water would be good. Thank you,' she tacked on belatedly. She hadn't meant to sound rude. Her whole mind was now focused on the job ahead. The most important performance of her life. Getting Matteo to sign the damned papers so she could finally move on—far, far away from him.

'Certainly, madam. This way.' The receptionist moved a little ahead of Skye, swishing her hips as she went, and Skye felt a momentary jab of envy for the other woman's curves. Skye had always been slim, but she'd desperately wanted larger breasts and hips when she was younger and had spent much of her teenage years stuffing her bras with tissues.

'Here we are,' the receptionist smiled, noticeably warmer now she knew to whom she was speaking, and stepped aside. 'He's waiting for you.'

Why did that conjure a very strong image of a wolf?

Because Matteo was all predator. All strong, ruthless, heartless predator.

And she'd been his prey.

Well, that was no longer the case.

Skye squared her shoulders defiantly, mentally bracing herself and straightening her spine, sucking in a deep breath which she hoped would bring courage.

Still, nothing could have prepared her for that moment. The moment when the door swung open and Matteo stood just inside it.

Nothing.

The air ceased to exist; it was sucked out and she stood in a vacuum. A space devoid of oxygen, gravity, reason and sense. There was just her and Matteo, her husband. Her beautiful, hyper-masculine, ruggedly handsome, lying, cheating husband.

Her throat was dry, her nerves quivering.

Strength be damned.

She wanted to run at him. But to kiss him? Or claw his eyes out? Probably, she realised with a sinking heart, the former. She wanted to wrap her arms around his neck and pull his head down, pull his mouth to hers, to greet him as though she still believed in love and happily ever after.

He looked good enough to eat. It was pure coincidence that he was wearing the suit she'd always loved—the navy-blue one that drew attention to his broad shoulders and dark tan. Her eyes lifted to his face: his square jawline with the stubble that was nothing to do with fashion and everything to do with his impatience with something as dull as shaving; higher, to his generous lips and patrician nose; to cheekbones that were firm and high, slashed into his face in a sign of his determination; and eyes that were so dark they were almost black but for the flecks of gold that glistened in their depths.

Eyes that were staring at her now, undertaking their own inspection, running down her body with the kind of passion and possession she had, once upon a time, found mesmerising and addictive. Eyes that missed nothing, that skated over her stiletto-clad feet, higher to her slim, bare legs and the floaty dress she wore that fell to just above her knees and covered her in a mysterious cloud of pale yellow fabric. Her arms were bare; he caught a glimpse of her wedding ring and grimaced.

Good.

Let him feel the awkwardness of this.

His eyes lifted higher to her face, roaming it freely…marking it for changes?

There were not many. In fact, Skye would have said she looked almost exactly as she had five weeks earlier when she'd left their house, their marriage, their life. All of her changes were internal, except for the heavy fringe she'd had cut a week or so earlier, having decided spontaneously that she needed a change. Some outward sign that she was no longer the same woman who'd been caught up in the Matteo Vin Santo Show.

She had grown up—a lot—in the short space of time. She barely recognised the woman she'd been. So naïve, stupid and so damned trusting!

'Thank you for seeing me,' she said, breaking the silence with a businesslike tone, pleased with how crisply she enunciated each syllable. 'I won't take up much of your time.'

Ah, how well she knew him! She saw the glint of sardonic mockery in his eyes and she resented him for that. His ability to make her feel foolish and immature even in this, the most adult of circumstances.

He said nothing, though, simply stepping deeper into the room, making room for her to enter his office. She did so with no degree of pleasure. She'd been in the room before, and her eyes fell to the table, taking in the very spot where she'd sat and started to sign the papers. The papers that had been the beginning of the end.

'You don't love me, do you?' She stared at the documents and then her husband as all the pieces of information came together. 'I asked my lawyer

about this. He told me everything. You. My dad. The whole sordid history. This is why you married me!'

His surprise was obvious and it infuriated Skye.

'You really didn't think I'd find out? You didn't think I'd ask about this?' She waved the contract in the air. 'It's all been about this damned hotel, hasn't it? A hotel my dad bought from your grandfather. A hotel you've been trying to buy back for fifteen years. My God! This is what our marriage is all about!'

Silence stretched between them. Silence that pulled, pulled and pulled at her nerve-ends until they snapped.

'We should talk about this later,' he said seriously. 'Just sign the papers and we'll go for dinner tonight.'

'Don't.' She slammed her palm down on the table. 'Don't you dare infantilise me! I deserve to know the truth. I want to hear it from your own mouth. This hotel is why you came to London. Why you met me. Right?'

His eyes narrowed and for a moment she wondered if he would say something to make this better, to alleviate the pain that was cracking through her soul.

'Yes.'

Skye's heart shook in her chest. She gripped

the chair-back for support. 'And why you married me?'

He was quiet for a long moment; it was a silence that tore her to shreds. And then he gave a simple, decisive nod that was the death knell to the fragile hopes she still held deep inside.

The memories were swirling through her, threatening to suck her back in time, but the door clicking shut jolted her into the present.

They were alone.

'Well, Skye, this is…unexpected.'

Her heart thumped painfully in her chest, ramming against her ribcage. God, his accent. How had she forgotten the sensual appeal of his husky, deep, Italian-edged voice?

Be strong. This will be over soon enough.

'You must have known I'd come back at some point,' she said with a shrug of her slender shoulders, pleased with how confident the words sounded, even as her fingers were shaking a little.

'I knew no such thing,' he countered. His accent was thicker—a sign of his fury, she knew. It was only in moments of deep emotional distress that this happened. 'You disappeared into thin air after you left my office without so much as the courtesy of a goodbye.'

Skye's caramel eyes flew wide. 'Courtesy? You want to talk about courtesy?'

His eyes narrowed warningly. 'I want to talk about where the hell you've been.'

'Like you care,' she said with a roll of her eyes.

'My wife disappeared, leaving no way to contact her. You think I don't care?'

'This is all about acquisition and ownership for you, isn't it? *Your* wife.' She shook her head angrily, realising that she was fighting a losing battle. 'I was in England,' she said on a sigh.

'Not at your house,' he said, and for a second her heart squeezed. Because it was proof he'd looked for her. Proof he'd tried to find her.

'No.' A rejection of that tenderness.

She knew why he'd looked for her and it had nothing to do with their sham marriage. He must have been furious to discover that she'd cancelled his purchase. That she'd found out about the pieces he'd been casually, secretly, manoeuvring through their short, disastrous marriage. Had he thought he could keep her so sensually fogged that she wouldn't wake up and realise what the hell was going on? He had almost been right. He'd come so close to taking the hotel from her without her even realising.

'Where were you?' he pushed, his own words hardened with something she knew to be anger. Because Matteo Vin Santo liked to win. He liked to win at all costs, and she'd found out just in time.

'It's none of your damned business.' She glared

at him now, the veneer of civility slipping away. She tried to grab it but being here with him, in this room, overpowered by how damned handsome he was, made something inside her snap.

'You're my wife,' he corrected, moving closer so that she caught a hint of his masculine fragrance. Her knees almost buckled. 'I have every right to know.'

But it was the wrong thing to say. His casual insistence of his rights fired every hint of anger in her body. 'That's outrageous.' Her eyes held the strength of steel when they locked with his. 'You have no rights. Not where I'm concerned.'

A muscle throbbed at the base of his jaw. 'You're my wife.' As though that explained everything!

'That's what I'm here to talk to you about,' Skye asserted forcefully in an attempt to regain control of the situation, reaching for her handbag at the same moment a sharp knock on the door preceded the interruption of the receptionist.

She brought a bottle of mineral water and a glass with ice cubes and a wedge of lemon into the room and placed them on the boardroom table.

'Thank you,' Skye murmured, relieved to have a form of distraction. She hoped it might calm her raging nerves. She twisted the lid, waiting for the hiss of bubbles to silence and the receptionist to leave the room, before tipping half the water into the glass.

'What, exactly, are you here to discuss?' he prompted, crossing his arms over his chest. She didn't need to look at him to know how broad that chest was. She lifted her mineral water and moved towards the window instead, staring down at Venice without really seeing it.

'Our marriage.' The words were a ghost. They conjured all the memories she wanted to forget.

The love-at-first-sight romance. The wedding itself. The way their marriage had been marked by nights of complete sensual abandon. Long days of waiting for him to come home hadn't mattered. She'd been so exhausted she'd napped and eaten, preparing for his return, and then she'd been his willing sex slave. Self-disgust at her stupidity gnawed at her gut.

She twisted the enormous diamond around her finger before sliding it off one last time. 'And how we're going to end it.' She spun round, her back to the view, her eyes landing squarely on his face, locking to his. She bravely held his gaze as she placed the ring on the boardroom table, then hastily stepped away from it as though it might burn her.

His expression was grim, but he said nothing initially. There was no shock. No outrage. No attempt to argue. To win her back.

Because it had never really been about her.

It had been about him, his grandfather, her father, and some stupid hotel she'd never even heard of. A vendetta that she knew nothing about which seemed to have controlled the lives of all those she'd loved. Her father, her husband…

Skye straightened her back, wounded pride forming the shield she needed.

'I have the divorce papers here,' she said softly. 'You just need to sign them and I'll take care of the rest.'

He expelled a breath; his expression gave little away. 'Show me.'

Skye could scarcely believe how well this was going! She'd been fretting about meeting Matteo again, yet he was being so reasonable… She told herself she was relieved.

'Here.' She pulled the document out of her handbag. It was only five pages long. She passed it to him, careful not to get too close, careful not to let their fingers touch.

His eyes, when they met hers, were scathing. He knew. He knew she was avoiding him.

He skimmed each sheet of paper, reading the words quickly, then placed them on the edge of his desk.

'And if I don't want to divorce you?'

Skye froze, the success she'd already been inwardly celebrating shattering. Her face drained of all colour. 'Don't be absurd.' The words were whispered from her before she remembered that she needed to be strong. Confident. Matteo preyed on weakness.

'What's absurd about wanting to stay married to you?'

And he strode across the room, closing the distance between them, his eyes locked to hers until she was quivering where she stood. Strength, apparently, deserted her at her moment of need.

'This wasn't a real marriage,' she muttered, standing her ground with effort. 'We both know that.'

His lips flicked with what she took to reflect silent agreement.

'It felt real enough to me.' The words were dangerously silky. His hand snaked around her waist, catching her completely by surprise. He jerked her against him, her softness meeting his hard strength in a way that was instantly familiar. Desire flooded her. Heat scorched her soul and a soft moan escaped her lips unbidden. It was foolish to stay so close to him, yet she did. She had denied herself this contact for long, miserable weeks, and now she wanted to enjoy it. Just for a moment. One last time.

'It wasn't,' she said huskily. 'I know that now.'

'What do you know?' The question was asked quietly. Almost gently

'I know everything.' She closed her eyes. 'I know about your father and my father. I know they fell in love with the same woman and your father married her. I know that my father was angry. I know that he went out of his way to hurt your family.' Her words cracked as she glossed over the admittance of her father's part in the angst. 'I know he felt hurt and rejected and that he took it out on you financially.'

Matteo's laugh was a grim rejection. 'You make it sound so sterile. Believe me, this was not the case.' He leaned forward, his expression menacing. 'Carey Johnson bankrupted my grandfather. Your father destroyed *everything* my grandfather spent a *lifetime* building.'

His vehement passion paralysed her for a moment, but belatedly she found her voice. 'And so you wanted to punish me?'

Silence fell around them, thick and caustic. She could see him weighing his words, carefully choosing what to say.

'It was never about punishing you,' he said finally.

'Punishing him, then? Punishing my dad?'

What could he say to that? Wasn't it the truth? Hadn't he delighted in the final insult he'd held over that bastard Carey Johnson? Making Skye moan for him, Matteo, in his bed all night long? Yes. He'd wanted to take his revenge, one sweet night at a time, and Skye had been a very obliging pawn in his game.

'You married me because you loved me.' He returned to their original point with apparent ease, the question asked silkily. 'Remember?'

God, she had loved him. She'd fallen for him, but it had all been an act. She noted dispassionately how he hadn't included his own feelings in the neat summation. His feelings were irrelevant; no, his feelings were *non-existent*. 'Love and hate are so close on the emotional spectrum, aren't they? It amazed me, too, how quickly that love morphed into something else.'

'You're saying you hate me?' he prompted, his free hand lifting to her hip, holding her where she was. She felt the stirring of his arousal and her breath snagged in her throat.

Sex.

That was the only truth of their marriage. Even he wasn't that good an actor. The desire had been real. It had controlled him as much as it had her.

'Of course I hate you,' she hissed, knowing she needed to pull away from him—that she would, in a moment. 'How could I feel anything else for you?'

His laugh was pure, sensual cynicism. 'Careful, *cara*. You and I both know how easy it would be for me to prove you a liar.' He rolled his hips, bringing his arousal into intimate contact with her body, and Skye felt a groan tear through her. Need, unmistakable and urgent, grew within her soul.

'That's just physical,' she hissed, her eyes locked to the top button of his crisp, pale blue shirt. 'And I'm sure you've had enough experience to know it doesn't mean a damned thing.'

'But you haven't,' he reminded her mercilessly, his eyes glowing with intensity. 'You were all mine.'

More memories. Their first time together—her first time with any man. She bit down on her lip, hating the way her nerves jerked in response. He'd taken hold of her that night, body and soul. He'd unlocked parts of her she hadn't even been aware of, and it had all been a part of his game. His plan for revenge. How easy she'd been to con into this marriage—into his bed!

'And I think you still are.'

A garbled sound escaped from Skye's throat. But it wasn't a denial. Was it a sound of surrender? Because he was right. She was desperate to feel his body once more. To be with him one last time.

He would probably always have that power over her, but *everything* hinged on her being able to stay strong. To remember the reason she had to get the papers signed and get the heck away from him. There was no future for them. There couldn't be. How could she stay married to a man she loved with all her heart, raise a baby with him, knowing that he'd used her in the most cynical of ways?

Her only hope was never to see him again. To go far from where he could find her. And that was her plan. Once he'd signed the papers she was going to disappear again. She thought of the ticket in her purse, a flight to Australia for later that night, where she planned to find her way to a remote corner of the country, somewhere with a view of the beach, and set about healing her broken heart.

'You're wrong.' She pulled away from him with determination, moving back to the window and staring out at Venice.

'Am I?'

'Oh, fine.' She shrugged her shoulders, not turning around. 'Apparently, I still…desire you. So what? You were my first lover. I dare say my body won't ever completely forget the lessons you taught me.' Fragments of their nights cut through her determination. The way he'd kissed her for hours; the way his mouth had owned her body. The way they'd swum naked in the moonlit ocean off the coast of Sicily or in the rooftop pool at his Venetian mansion. The sensual massages he'd given her. She pushed those thoughts aside. 'But nor will my heart.'

'And what did I teach your heart, *cara*?'

'Not to trust handsome strangers,' she said, the humour of the comment sucked away by the desperation in her voice. 'Sign the papers, Matteo. This marriage is over.'

'And if I won't?' The words were thick with emotion. And for a second hope scorched her. But it was a foolish hope, the same blind love that had led her into the marriage.

'You wanted revenge. You got it.'

'I wanted the hotel,' he said with a dangerous softness to his voice. 'You were…a silver lining.'

'A silver lining?' she returned angrily. 'For God's sake, Matteo. I *loved* you! Doesn't that mean anything to you?'

He stared at her long and hard. 'That wasn't love you felt. It was infatuation. Sex.'

She swallowed past a lump of bitterness in her throat. He was wrong. She'd loved him with her whole heart. She wouldn't tell him that now, but somehow knowing that their baby had been conceived with goodness in her heart, at least, mattered a whole lot to her.

'Perhaps you're right,' she said with an attempt at a nonchalant shrug. 'It's all academic now. Our marriage is over. There's obviously no way on earth I could ever forget what you've done. Nor forgive you for it.' She sucked in a breath and stared at him headlong. 'You can have the hotel.'

He was instantly still, every nerve ending in his body in a state of stasis. 'You're saying you'll sell me Il Grande Fortuna?'

'On one condition,' she said frostily, devastation at this final, damning proof seeping into her blood, turning it to ice. 'Sign the damned papers and stay the hell out of my life.'

When Skye had walked out on their marriage, having learned the truth behind his motivations for pursuing her, he'd had to reconcile himself to the reality that he might never recover his grandfather's beloved Il Grande Fortuna.

He'd put all his chips on the one square, gambling on marriage to the rich heiress as the best way to get what he wanted. And to have a little fun along the way.

His plan had been simple enough—seduce her and blind her with the passion they shared, making her willing to do, say or sign anything he asked of her. And he'd come so close. She had been eating out of the palm of his hand. Until she wasn't.

Their marriage had always been about the hotel.

About returning his family's property to its rightful owner—him.

It had been about righting a wrong of the past.

About avenging his *nonno*.

Hell, he'd married her because it had been the

only way to get the hotel back into his family's trust. Now she was giving him the thing he'd wanted all his adult life on a silver platter, yet he found himself hesitating.

Why the hell wasn't he just agreeing to her terms?

Because he didn't like to concede defeat. And, even though he'd have the hotel, he didn't like the idea of Skye walking away from him before he was ready.

'Sign the divorce papers, Teo.' She used the diminutive form of his name by mistake. The way her face paled showed her remorse. That wasn't who they were any more. Hell, they'd never been that couple. Not really.

He'd never even wanted a wife. He'd wanted the hotel, and their marriage had been the clearest way to achieve that aim, but Matteo Vin Santo was a bachelor from way back. If he signed this paper, he'd be rid of the wife he'd never really wanted and he'd have the hotel. The only thing to regret was that he wouldn't have the pleasure of his wife's body again. A small price to pay for achieving a decades-old goal, though. 'Fine.' His nod was curt.

Her relief was palpable. He tried not to take it personally. She'd be all kinds of stupid to want anything other than a divorce from him—and Skye Johnson was definitely not stupid.

'But I have a condition of my own.'

Her brows shot up, her lips parted, and he ached to kiss her. To wipe that look of disdain from her pretty features. To remind her of just how she came apart in his arms. He'd always loved her in yellow. It showed off her flawless honey skin, the darkness of her hair, the innocence of who she was.

'I want one more night with you.'

Skye froze, her eyes sweeping shut, her lips parting wider as she struggled for breath. He watched the words take effect; the way colour spread through her cheeks.

'No.' It was just a whisper. A husky denial. 'Never.'

He laughed, a harsh sound of cynicism and frustration. 'Never say never, *cara*. Not when you fall apart in my arms as you do...'

Skye tilted her chin, her eyes locked defiantly with his.

'Desire is one thing, but I have no intention of acting on it.'

'Then I have no intention of signing those papers,' he threatened silkily.

Panic flooded her. *Fascinating.*

'What's the matter? Is the idea of being Mrs Matteo Vin Santo so abhorrent to you? I remember a time when you couldn't wait to be my wife—and be in my bed.'

'I didn't know who you were then. Nor what you were capable of.'

'And what am I capable of?'

'It doesn't matter.' Haunted, miserable words that slammed against him. Guilt was not something Matteo had much experience of, but he felt a flush of it. He didn't like it.

His obligation was to his family.

Not Skye.

But her hurt was obvious and it was a hurt he had caused.

Yes, he felt guilt. He felt remorse. He wished… what? That he could change it? That he could have procured the hotel without hurting her?

It wasn't possible. He'd tried that. He'd spent years trying to lure her father into selling and the bastard had been determined.

'Over my dead body.' Those were the last words Carey Johnson had said to Matteo. If Carey had only listened to reason, if he hadn't been driven by the stupid grudge that had led to his taking the hotel in the first instance, it would never have come to this.

But, looking across his office at his wife, Matteo wasn't sure he cared about the hotel, his grandfather or her father. None of them mattered. He wasn't foolish enough to think he could salvage their marriage—nor did he believe he wanted to. But he needed, desperately, to kiss her.

To touch her.

To wipe away the grief that was saturating her slender frame.

Like he used to, as though it were his God-given right to hold her in his arms. They were tinder and flame—together the effect had always been extraordinary.

'Don't.' Her eyes held a warning. 'Don't look at me like that.'

'Like what?' He moved closer, just a few steps, and there was still a table between them. Her ring caught his eye and he reached for it without realising, fingering its weight in his hand, remembering the day he'd bought it. He'd deliberately chosen something enormous, thinking it would be exactly what she would want. The heiress of the Johnson fortune surely valued enormity and extravagance over all else?

Only it had never really suited her. Over the weeks of their short marriage, he'd begun to imagine what he should have chosen instead. Something slender with an understated elegance, made of rose-gold and inlaid diamonds. Perhaps onyx, to match her hair.

He swallowed past the thought. It was a distraction, a red herring. What he needed was to remember the hotel. To remember the reason he'd done all of this.

'Don't look at me like you're actually sorry this

is happening. Like you didn't expect it.' She tilted her chin. 'Like this has anything to do with you and me.'

'It *is* our marriage we're discussing ending.'

'Marriage!' She spat the word and his gut rolled. It was as though a blade had been plunged through him. Her anger and disbelief filled the room. 'This was *never* a marriage! It was a damned trick. A machination. Nothing more. You win, okay? You win! Take the hotel! I don't want it. I don't want anything that will ever remind me of you!' Her voice was loud. He'd put bets on his receptionist Anastasia having heard every word but he didn't care.

Skye's pain was palpable and he longed to kiss her to wipe it away. It was the only way he could think of to remove the ache from her eyes; the tears that glistened on her lashes were tiny, moist recriminations that landed squarely in his chest.

'How you must have loved the knowledge that you had such a sweet revenge over my father! How you'd done something he would have hated, something I would *never* have agreed to if I'd known about your feud. How you must have been *laughing* at me! Every night when you came home you found me so happy to see you, and all the while you were lining up the pieces, getting ready to finally swoop.'

A muscle jerked on the hard ridge of his jaw. 'Yes, Skye. I'm only human. Do you want me to lie to you now? To tell you that our marriage had nothing to do with the fact your father was the biggest bastard on earth? That the fact I hated him with every fibre of my being didn't have anything to do with why I married you?'

She held a hand up. Her fingers were shaking and her face was so pale that, momentarily, he felt a clutch of anxiety for her. She looked terrible; ill. Matteo was torn between anger at the situation and a strange concern for his wife.

Tears spilled out of her eyes now, rolling down her cheeks. She was so weary. All the planning and coping had taken its toll, and she was utterly exhausted. It showed in the tremble of her voice and the grey of her cheeks. 'No. There's nothing you can say that I want to hear. In fact, I can't bear to be in the same room as you for a moment longer. Just sign the divorce papers. Please. Take the hotel and leave me alone.' She bit down on her lip as she tried to keep her sobbing at bay.

It was everything he'd wanted. He'd come to accept that he would never get the hotel back—not once Skye had learned the truth. And here she was, offering it to him on a silver platter just to be rid of him.

Was that it? Was his pride wounded by her desperation to be free of their marriage? Was that why he wanted to rail against her insistence? To remind her of what they'd shared—physically— one last time?

His eyes dropped to the divorce papers and then lifted with a heavy grimness towards her face. 'Fine. If that's what you want.'

'I never want to see you again.'

The heat of Venice slapped her in the face as soon as she stepped out of his office. It was early afternoon and the city was packed. Workers were jostling along the street, tourists were busy taking photographs and Skye was in the midst of them, surprise at what she'd just accomplished moving through her.

She took a step towards the crowds, her mind numb. What now?

Her breath was shallow.

Shock, she supposed, reaching for a pillar to support her. Stars flew in her eyes and heat spread through her body followed by weakness and an odd, soul-deep exhaustion.

It was over.

She was free.

Her hand pressed to her stomach and another wave of tiredness hit her. She didn't want anything to do with Matteo, but she was going to raise their baby. Could she do it and never think of him?

She'd have to. Matteo was in her past and this baby was her future.

The baby was all that mattered.

She sucked in a breath, but it didn't seem to reach her lungs.

'Eh, you okay, miss?'

A kindly gondola operator lifted his brows, waiting for an answer, so she nodded, even though she wasn't sure she was. 'Just hot,' she said, fanning her face.

But the simple, tiny exertion of moving her hand up and down was the straw that broke the camel's back. Darkness enveloped her.

CHAPTER TWO

MATTEO WASN'T LOOKING out of the window in the hope of seeing her. He'd simply been standing and staring in that direction ever since she'd left. Really, he was barely aware of the flow of traffic in and out along the busy tourist strip.

He saw Skye.

The anguish on her features.

The pain of her heart that she wore so visibly.

He'd used her, and that hadn't bothered him. Causing pain to her had been something he'd been more than willing to gamble. It was her own father's fault—if Skye was hurt, it was because of Carey Johnson's intractable bull-headedness.

But he hadn't banked on witnessing her pain. He hadn't enjoyed that. He was a driven business-man, not an out-and-out bastard. Witnessing the tears gliding down her soft, pale cheeks, the ac-cusation in her eyes…he hadn't been prepared for how that would gut him. How it would make him feel unpleasantly remorseful, even when he knew he would make all the same decisions over again, given the chance.

He lifted his fingers to his chin, rubbing the

stubble there, before a commotion dragged his attention down to ground level.

It was the pastel yellow of her dress that caught his eye first. The way it seemed to crumple as she fell, her body, slender and unmistakable, toppling backwards. She fell as she did everything—with grace.

It was the work of a moment. Skye was collapsing, then she was dropping over the edge of the railing into the murky, germ-infested waters of Venice. Had he stayed still a little longer, he would have seen the moment her head cracked against the side of a gondola.

But he didn't.

Adrenalin galvanised him.

Matteo ran from his office faster than he'd known was possible, tearing through the foyer and bursting onto the footpath just as a gondola operator in his distinctive black-and-white-striped shirt dived into the water. The dress made her easy to spot. Though Matteo could see the boatswain had wrapped an arm around her waist, he couldn't stand idly by. Instincts alone drove his actions. A gentle ribbon of blood swirled through the water; he dove through it.

'Is she breathing?' Matteo pulled Skye to him, holding her as he swam to the edge of the canal. A crowd had formed and someone held their hands down, urging Matteo to lift her out. He passed her body up, then climbed out himself.

She was so peaceful. As though she were asleep. More blood.

It seeped onto the pavement beneath her head and he gently fingered her scalp, a grim line on his mouth. 'Call a water ambulance,' he demanded, used to being obeyed and not doubting for one second that someone would do as he'd commanded.

'One is on its way,' someone replied.

Thank God. He crouched down beside her, running a hand over her face. 'You're okay, *cara*. You're going to be fine.'

He had the vague impression of the gondola operator being helped out of the water, but his entire focus was on Skye. He spoke to her softly in his own language, urging her to wake up, not to worry, to trust him, knowing that if she'd been awake she'd have thrown that invitation back in his face.

It was only minutes before the scream of a water ambulance heralded its arrival, but it felt like a lot longer as Matteo stared down at her ashen face and wondered just what the hell had happened to make her fall into the filthy waters of Venice. The water ambulance pulled to a hasty stop beside them and two men began to call orders to the crowd. They climbed up nearby steps and ran to Skye, lifting her onto a flimsy backboard.

'You're with her?' one of them asked Matteo.

He nodded. 'I'm her…husband.'

'You can come, then.'

He could have laughed at the medic's apparent belief that he had any say in Matteo Vin Santo's actions. Matteo paused for the briefest moment, just long enough to toss a thick pile of soggy bank notes at the gondola operator with a quick word of thanks, and then he followed behind.

The speedboat, bright yellow and sleek, accommodated Skye on a bed, and he watched her as the boat made its way speedily through Venice.

Only twice during the trip did her eyes open, and both times she looked at him with a mixture of confusion and non-comprehension.

The boat pulled up at the *ospedale* dock and there was a medical team waiting.

It all happened so quickly. She was admitted after a cursory examination, and there was enough concern on the nurse's face to make Matteo wonder if she was gravely ill.

'What's going on?' he asked, once she was ensconced in her own room.

No one answered. They were all busy working, checking her vital signs, rolling her onto her side and inspecting her head, checking for the damage that was causing the bleeding. A nurse drew several vials of blood and raced them from the room.

And then he was waiting, standing beside her bed, wondering what had happened, wondering if she'd be okay.

After an interminable time, a woman in a white coat entered the room and moved towards Matteo, her smile reassuring. 'She is your wife?'

He nodded. 'Yes.' The word was hardened by years of being in command. Of calling the shots and asking the questions. 'How is she?'

'She's had a bump to the head, but it doesn't look too serious. Unfortunately, the tests we'd usually run to be sure are obviously impossible at the moment. She may be a little groggy when she wakes, possibly for a day or so. I don't anticipate any other complications, though.'

None of her words eased Matteo's concern. 'What happened to her?'

'My guess would be that she passed out. It's not unusual, in her condition. The heat of the day wouldn't have helped—'

'Wait a moment,' he said, lifting a hand to stop her. 'What condition?'

The doctor pulled a face. 'You don't know?'

'Know what, *dottore*?'

'About the baby?'

The world stopped spinning. No. It lurched catastrophically off its axis, sucking Matteo with it. He was in freefall as the doctor's words filtered through his mind. 'What baby?' he asked, the question gravelled.

'Your wife is pregnant. It's very early stages—it's quite by accident that the nurse even tested for it. Does she know?'

Hell.

Matteo's eyes were dragged to Skye, still so peaceful-looking. Despite the fact her dark hair was matted around her, her eyes were shut and she looked serene. Had she known?

I never want to see you, ever *again.*

A muscle clenched in his jaw. Had she really been planning to divorce him and keep their child from him?

An ache spread through him, an ache of misery and disbelief. Of anger and rage. Skye wasn't capable of that deception, surely?

She *couldn't* have known.

'She hadn't mentioned it,' he said with a hint of the ruthless determination that had seen him rebuild a once-great empire from its ashes and ruins. But his mind was reeling. Shock was seeping through him.

Skye was pregnant? And she'd come to him, seeking a divorce? A divorce he'd agreed to because he'd known he owed her that much; because he'd wanted her to be happy. And he'd thought he was done making stupid, emotion-driven decisions!

Would Skye have insisted on a divorce if she'd known about the baby? He couldn't believe it of his wife. And yet, she was the daughter of that bastard Johnson. Did he really have any idea what she was capable of?

His brow was fevered as he replayed every detail of their meeting, looking for signs that she knew her condition. Had she touched her stomach at all? What else would a pregnant woman do? He had no clue.

Hell.

The idea of a baby had never even really occurred to him; foolish, given how often they'd come together.

'Perhaps she has not been symptomatic.' The doctor shrugged, as though it didn't matter. As though it weren't the most important news Matteo had received in his life. As though Skye's knowledge or lack thereof wouldn't change *everything*.

How could he forgive her if she'd planned to keep it from him?

His nod was distracted. 'Is the baby okay?'

'So far as I can tell.' The doctor smiled reassuringly.

They'd only ever talked about children briefly. Skye was too young to have been thinking of having babies and Matteo hadn't entered into the marriage with procreation on his mind. But still!

She must have known how much this child would mean to him.

And she'd been intending to take the Vin Santo heir away from him. To raise his child as a Johnson!

Fury whipped at the soles of his feet, spurring him forward. 'Did my wife's handbag…?'

'Yes, I believe it was dropped off separately.' The doctor nodded curtly. 'Someone found it on the pavement.'

His expression was grim.

'I'll have it brought in.'

'Thank you.'

He waited impatiently, staring at Skye, trying to make sense of this, trying to hold his temper together. But, the more time that passed, the more he came to suspect the worst.

She'd been so adamant about the divorce— that it had to be right now. She had no time to wait.

And she'd held out the perfect carrot to get him to fit in with her plans! The hotel! The damned hotel. He would have done anything to get it back, even marrying her. And, yes, even divorcing her.

He'd wanted the matter of their marriage and the hotel resolved and she'd given him that on a platter. What a fool he was! He'd almost let go of the most valuable thing in his life.

His child.

How could he have been so stupid? Hadn't he learned his lesson with the whole Maria debacle? He'd just been a boy then. A young, foolish boy. He'd fallen for her lies hook, line and sinker. He'd fallen in love with her too. And learned how stupid a notion love was. He'd sworn he'd never trust a woman again, and here he'd been about to take Skye's request at face value. Damn it! She was a Johnson, first and foremost. When had he forgotten that?

A hospital staffer arrived minutes later, handing the handbag to him in a large plastic bag.

He took it without speaking, reaching for her bag and ripping it open. There were the damned divorce documents, alongside his purchase contract on the hotel. He removed both angrily and stuffed them in the still-damp pocket of his suit.

He was about to drop the bag to the floor when something else caught his eye.

Curiously, he reached for it, and his anger only darkened when he saw that the object was her passport with a ticket folded neatly inside. A quick inspection showed that it was to take her to Sydney, Australia, later that night.

The evidence was truly damning. All doubt evaporated and left inside him a seed of anger so powerful that it ripped his soul in half.

She had been going to take this child from him. His flesh and blood.

Nausea rolled through him, rising in his chest. He gripped his hands together, his eyes resting on his wife's face—so beautiful, even like this.

Had she truly wanted to raise a child away from him? Without him ever even knowing?

The pain at the very idea was sharp.

'Signor Vin Santo? We have spare clothes if you would like to get changed.' A nurse was smiling at him kindly.

He didn't return it. He couldn't. 'I'll stay with my *wife*, thank you.' The words rang with derision, yet the nurse didn't seem to detect the undercurrent of Matteo's tension.

Fury was at war with disbelief.

A machine was rolled through the door, its wheels making a soft squeaking noise as it was brought to rest beside Skye. The doctor he'd been speaking to earlier bustled in and sent him a look of reassurance.

'Try not to be so worried,' she said, pushing Skye's dress up and arranging the blankets around her hips, exposing only her stomach. It was so flat. Was it possible that the doctor had got it wrong? How could a baby be developing inside her tiny frame?

His eyes devoured her body once more, purposefully looking for changes now. Her neat breasts were still small and round, just enough to fill his palms. But perhaps there was a new roundness to them he hadn't appreciated before...

He swallowed past the bitterness. He would process her betrayal later. Once he knew his baby was okay.

The doctor lifted a part of the machine and pressed it to Skye's belly, and Skye made a soft moaning noise.

'Is it painful?' Matteo asked instinctively.

'No, not at all.' The doctor spun the cart around so that Matteo could see the screen. He lifted his eyes to it and frowned.

'What am I looking at?'

'It's too early to see anything clearly. I would say she is perhaps six weeks.' The doctor smiled at him kindly. 'Your baby is around the size of a lentil.'

'A lentil?'

'A legume,' she clarified. 'But I can see good blood-flow generally. There's nothing here that worries me.' She went to lift the wand but Matteo spoke, arresting her movement.

'What is that?' He pointed to a line at the bottom of the screen.

'Ah. That is the heartbeat.'

'The heartbeat?' He closed his eyes as the reality began to thunder through him.

Emotions gripped him, so strong, so raw, and

suddenly he wasn't capable of speech. He stepped away from the bed, from his wife, from the doctor, and sucked in a deep breath of air.

'Why don't you get changed, Signor Vin Santo? You'll be no help to her if you've come down with a flu.'

He didn't answer. He was busy analysing the situation, trying to make sense of it.

Skye was pregnant with his child. With the Vin Santo heir. And she'd wanted to keep the information from him.

Unless... He turned slowly, his eyes locked to the doctor's. Hope briefly flared in his chest. 'You asked if she knew. Is there any way she *wouldn't* have known?'

The doctor's empathy was palpable. 'Of course. It is still very early. If she hasn't mentioned it to you, I think it is highly likely that she didn't yet realise. It really depends on whether she had any other symptoms, and if she had a reason to do a pregnancy test. Were you trying to conceive?'

'No.' Their marriage was about one thing, and one thing only. The hotel. A child would just have complicated matters further.

How the hell had this even happened? She'd been on the pill, hadn't she?

'Your wife will be awake soon.' The doctor leaned over and lifted one of Skye's eyelids, then nodded confidently. 'You will be able to ask her.'

It was suddenly imperative for Matteo to know the truth. No, it was imperative for him to know that she *hadn't* known. He couldn't believe that Skye would have planned to keep this information from him. Despite the evidence against her, he still had hope. A part of him believed she would never do something as calculated as taking a baby from its father.

No matter what he'd done, no matter what she believed, this was *different*. Their baby was not a pawn; it deserved better than to be used by either of them as a bargaining chip.

But worse was the belief she hadn't intended to use it as a bargaining chip at all. Worse was the realisation that she had simply meant to disappear. To get on a plane and fly out of his life, taking his son or daughter with her.

He ground his teeth together and turned back to the bed.

His heart rolled.

It wasn't possible.

'Matteo? Where am I?'

Her thin, raspy voice drew his attention. He stared at her long and hard before speaking. 'You're in the hospital. In Venice.' His expression was guarded, but he felt anger in his every expression, beneath the mask of civility he had donned with effort.

'Hospital?' Her eyes swept shut. 'I fell. No, I fainted. That happens sometimes.'

'Since when?' he demanded icily, moving closer.

Her hands dropped to her stomach and he could see that she was in turmoil, that she was agonising over what to say. But apparently a need for reassurance eclipsed all other concerns. 'Is he okay? Is my baby okay?'

CHAPTER THREE

EVERY SOUND IN the hospital was audible. The beeping of far-away machines monitoring the life signs of patients. The low-key chat of staff. The ringing of a phone. The whir of an overhead fan. Everything was audible in that way when things take on an almost supersonic quality in moments of shock and duress. The sounds had a brightness beyond their due.

Skye waited, her breath held, her worry lurching desperately.

'Matteo?' It was a whisper. A strangled, hoarse cry. 'Please tell me...'

'Our baby is fine,' he said with a coldness that perforated her relief and doused it in ice.

Skye's eyes fell closed. The whole point of coming to Italy and forcing his hand, of giving him the hotel, had been to ensure they were divorced before it was too late. Before her stomach became rounded, before she had given birth to their child, before he had any concept there even was a child. But she wasn't sure she could summon the energy to care in that moment.

None of that mattered.

She felt only relief.

Tears stung her eyes. 'Thank God. Oh, Matteo, I'm so relieved.'

'They're going to monitor you,' he said, taking a step back from the bed and crossing his arms. 'For a few more hours.'

'I'm fine.' Skye reached for the IV cable that was attached to her wrist and pulled it out. Matteo winced as the inch-long needle fell from her arm. 'Fainting is one of the symptoms I'm learning to live with.'

She stood, but was so unsteady that Matteo couldn't help but reach for her. His touch was clinical, but he didn't want to see his wife—no, the mother of his child—splayed across the bed, unconscious again.

'I'm fine,' she reiterated snappishly, and her teeth were bared, her body language the definition of defensive. But it was the behaviour of a badly wounded lioness defending her cub.

She was *terrified*.

Of him? Of his anger? Of what she thought he'd do? So she should be! To attempt to conceal the Vin Santo heir from him… Just who did she think he was? 'So you obviously knew you were pregnant.' The words held a latent threat.

She winced and pulled back, moving away from him by skirting the bed.

'When the hell were you planning on telling me?'

'Would you *stop* yelling?' she murmured.

Matteo ran his hand through his hair, pulling at it with barely suppressed frustration. He hadn't intended to yell; only a rage he hadn't felt for many years, since the last time he'd come up against a Johnson in a confrontation, had completely usurped all his other impulses. He spoke more softly, but there was an inherent danger to the silky edges of his words. 'You weren't going to tell me, were you?'

Skye looked at him for a moment and then turned her attention back to the bed. 'I didn't... feel it was any of your business,' she said, and somehow managed to look confidently defiant even as she extolled the absurd explanation.

'My baby is none of my business?' he responded with scathing disbelief. 'How exactly do you figure?'

'You don't want a child. Not with me. I was doing you a favour.' She shook her head. 'I was doing us *all* a favour. I don't want to raise a baby with you any more than you do with me. And the baby deserves to be born into a world that's not... full of bitterness and acrimony.'

'The baby deserves a chance to know both his parents,' Matteo responded sharply. 'You were going to deny both it and me that opportunity. Weren't you?'

She glared at him. 'You went into this marriage

wanting one thing, and one thing only. And now you have it. Children were no part of this.'

'*That* is beside the point. You are, in fact, pregnant with my child. This is not in the realms of the hypothetical. I had a right to know.'

Her mouth dropped open and she stared at him, searching for something to say—anything—that might explain her point of view.

The hurt she'd felt at realising that he'd used her. The fact that he'd conned her into falling in love with him, had used her inexperience and desire against her, knowing that he would never be able to give her the only thing she really wanted.

Love.

Matteo wasn't built to love. She knew that now. The newspapers that declared him heartless and ruthless were right.

What a fool she'd been to believe that their similar upbringings had destined them to be together. As though both having suffered the misfortune of being orphaned meant they would live happily ever after.

How could she explain to him that this option had been the best for everyone?

No words came to mind. Nothing. She had thought about it long and hard, though. She'd agonised over what to do. And this had made complete sense.

It *still* made sense.

'I don't want to raise a child with you,' she said with a determination that was somewhat belied by her quivering lower lip.

'That is not your decision.'

Skye pulled a face. 'We're divorced, remember? Or as good as.'

Matteo's mouth formed a grim line. 'There will be no divorce.' He reached into his pocket and pulled out the papers, tearing them in half with satisfaction, along with the contract for the hotel. The whole deal was off. This baby changed everything.

Skye's eyes followed the soft ripping of the soggy paper then flew to his face. 'You will not be flying out of Italy, taking my child with you.'

'You can't stop me,' she snapped, wrapping her arms around her slender body, holding herself tight.

'Like hell I can't.' He spoke coldly. 'If necessary I will take this matter to the family courts today.'

Skye's mouth dropped open. 'You…can't stop me from leaving. No court would make a mother remain in a country that she's not even a born citizen of.'

He lifted a hand, silencing her with the simple gesture. 'Perhaps not. But you had better believe I will have every reporter available covering the story. Our child will know, from as soon as he can read, that I fought *like a dog* for him. That I wanted him—and you wanted simply to take him from me.' He leaned closer, his face only inches from Skye's. 'I will fight for him with my dying breath. You will long for the days when we were married, rather than being in constant custody disputes in court.'

She shivered, his threat making her stomach roll. 'You wouldn't do it. You're too private.'

'There is *nothing* I wouldn't do for my child.'

'Then let-let me raise him,' Skye stammered. 'Let me raise our baby, because that's best for everyone. And you can be…involved,' she conceded, because she could clearly see she had no other option.

'How involved?' Matteo demanded.

'You can visit. Several times a year. I suppose I can bring him to Italy when he's older. We'll work out a schedule.' She said the word as though it was the miracle cure they desperately needed. 'Christmas, birthdays, just like every other divorced couple.'

'*Your* parents weren't together,' Matteo said with cold disbelief. 'You told me that you hated feeling pulled from one to the other. Yet you'd suggest it for our child?'

Skye froze. He was right, of course. Though Skye hadn't spoken much about her upbringing, she'd obviously given enough indication for him to glean the truth of her loneliness.

'We'll do it better than they did,' she said softly.

'We won't do it that way at all.'

Disbelief scored her heart. 'You can't make me stay married to you. That's insane.'

'Insane is what you planned to do. Insane is planning to hide your pregnancy and baby from me. Hell, Skye, I cannot believe you thought, for one moment, that I wouldn't find out.'

'How would you have?' she snapped. 'This was just bad luck. If I hadn't passed out…'

His eyes glittered with anger. 'Yes?'

Skye's cheeks were pale. 'You would never have known. Ever.'

'Because you were going to disappear into thin air and hide from me?' He moved closer, his expression menacing. 'And what if you met another man? Would you have married him? Raised my child with him? Would you have let my child, the Vin Santo heir, grow up with no idea of who he is? From where he comes?'

Skye was as white as a sheet and, in the part of Matteo's brain that was working, he recognised that he should ease up. That he should give her a moment to breathe and reach her own conclusions. Only, Matteo had rebuilt the family empire by sheer determination alone and easing up on any of his adversaries was not something he believed in doing.

And Skye *was* his adversary—his enemy—not just by blood, but now also by deed. How could she not be, given the deception she'd been willing to practice?

'Answer me, damn it!' he demanded, and when she didn't respond he grabbed her around the waist, pulling her body to his. Her lips parted on a wave of shock and he took advantage of the surprise, driven by a soul-deep instinct. He ground his mouth to hers, lashing her with his tongue, stirring her into the kind of frenzy that had typified their short, superheated marriage.

It wasn't just about possessing her. He wanted to possess all of her, to mark his claim on her as his wife, and as the mother of his baby. He wanted to claim their child. 'This is my baby.'

Skye was frozen with shock but it didn't last long. The second Matteo's lips touched hers she was flashing back into the past through the days of their marriage, the nights of their passion, the need that had always defined them. She was losing a battle to the only truth she could rely on—sensual need.

'Would you have raised him with another man?' He asked the question straight into her mouth so that she heard the words in the depths of her soul and felt his pain as though he'd touched her there. But he didn't break their kiss, making it difficult for Skye to answer.

'This is my child.' The statement was filled with judgement. 'And you are my wife.'

Skye made another sound, a mix between a groan and a sob, a sound of desperate emotion and pain, of acknowledgement and regret.

'I won't let you go. Not now.'

His hands moved inwards, finding her still-flat stomach. He ran his fingers over her and he ended their kiss, moving away, looking at her with eyes that were cold despite the raging intimacy they'd just shared. Despite the heat in Skye's blood, her cheeks, the awareness that fired in every part of her body.

'Come home with me.'

It was not a question, yet Skye still wanted to fight. 'It won't work.'

Matteo's eyes glittered. 'Of course it will.'

'Because our last attempt at marriage was such a success?' Skye scoffed, turning away from him so that she could take a moment to get her blood pressure under control, so that he wouldn't see the way she was trembling.

'I will not let you take my child from me. I will raise it on my own, or you can choose to be a part of his life.'

'How c-can you even say that?' she stammered,

spinning around to face him head on. 'No court would *ever* award you full custody!'

Matteo's eyes narrowed. 'Do you know who I am?'

A shiver ran down her spine; adrenalin pumped in her body.

'Do you know what I will do to get what I want?'

Skye's heart stammered in her chest. He'd married her for a stupid piece of real estate—an ancient hotel long since shut down; a building in the middle of Rome in which she had no interest. Matteo's determination to get what he wanted was indeed a force to be reckoned with.

To underscore his intent, he added, 'I will not rest until my child is in my home, being raised by me. Here. In Venice, where he belongs. For more than a thousand years, Skye, Vin Santos have lived on this island.' He pointed downwards, as if to indicate the ancient marshes on which the city was built. 'We are as much a part of Venice as Venice is of us. The child you carry in your womb is of me, of Venice, and this is where he should be. I will not let you take him.'

Skye shook her head, but fear was filling her all the way to the top of her heart.

Was he right? Could he, in fact, take their baby?

She needed to speak to a lawyer, and fast.

'If you fight me, I will spare no expense and I

will stop at nothing.' His teeth were bared, his expression vibrating with passionate resolve. 'I will make your life hell, and you will wish, one day, that you'd never met me. And that you'd never had my child.'

Skye was shaking. She was furious! She closed the distance between them on autopilot, lifting a hand and cracking it across his cheek.

'How dare you?' she demanded heatedly, watching as red spread across his cheek from where flesh had connected—hard—with flesh.

'I told you,' he said with a look of cold indifference. 'I will stop at *nothing* to get what I want.'

'And you want our child,' she said, turning her face away, looking towards the door of the hospital.

'*Si.*' Silence cracked between them, angry and vicious. Matteo broke it, forcing himself to be completely honest. To lay out for his wife the truth of their situation. 'But I also want you.'

Skye's stomach flopped instinctively—reflexively—against her judgement and certainly without her consent. 'Why?'

'Because you are my wife,' he said with a shrug, as though it made complete sense. 'And I like that you are my wife. I want you back in my bed, like you should have been all along. There is a silver lining to this mess, no?'

'God, Matteo! How can you think about sex

right now? How can you think I'd ever climb back into your *bed* after this? You're blackmailing me in the most hateful way! And I hate you! I hate you!'

'Yes,' he said with a decisive nod, his eyes narrowing. 'But are you not the one who said that hate and love are easily interchanged?'

'I will *never* be dumb enough to love you again. You disgust me.'

His laugh was a sharp dismissal. 'You desire me. Hate does not disqualify lust. *Si?*'

Shame flooded Skye. How could it be true? How could she feel such a strong physical attraction to Matteo, even after all that she knew of him? This man was a total bastard—he was nothing like the man she'd thought she'd married. He'd used her then and he was using her now.

She had very little pride left. And suddenly she had very little will to fight. She lifted her eyes to his, but there was a lingering shred of defiance in them from deep within her. 'Hell will freeze over before I sleep with you again.'

His laugh was mocking. 'You'll be begging me to take you in no time.' He dropped his mouth to hers. 'And I'm going to enjoy it, Mrs Vin Santo.'

There was anger in the depths of her toffee-coloured eyes. 'I swear to you, Matteo, I will never beg for you again.'

His laugh was dismissive. 'We'll see.'

* * *

Skye toyed with the necklace, pulling it from side to side, sliding the small locket from one slender shoulder to the other as she stared out at the setting sun.

She wondered, absentmindedly, if her flight had already left. Without her on it, taking with it her dreams of escape. Of freedom. Of a whole new world and life far, far away from Matteo Vin Santo and all his lies.

It was strange being back in the villa. Nothing had changed, yet everything was different.

The last time she'd been here, it had been with an air of delight. With pleasure, excitement. adoration and love. With lust, too. She had been a newlywed and life had been so simple. For, what reason could her powerful billionaire husband have for tricking her into marriage? They were both independently wealthy; he was a renowned ladies' man and there had been no advantage to him in marrying someone like her unless he'd fallen as utterly head over heels in love as she had.

And that had been so easy to believe!

He'd played the part perfectly. How could she have been so fooled by him? He had looked at her and everything had made sense. How had he not felt that?

Her stomach lurched as she remembered their wedding night. The beautiful anticipation of that

moment of first possession. For the month they'd
dated, he'd insisted on waiting, despite the fact
she'd begged him to take her night after night
after night.

She saw it now for what it was—another part
of his callous, calculated plan. He'd manipulated
her inexperience and desire. She had been the
one who'd pushed for a quick engagement. He'd
withheld the sexual satisfaction she'd been desperate for, knowing it would lead to a fast-track
wedding.

What was that expression? Marry in haste, re-
pent at leisure...

To be back in his house, pregnant with his baby,
still wanting him but so completely out of love...
What a nightmare it was.

Worse, he was right. His body still had the
power to make all her will-power crumble. How
she hated him for that!

A noise behind her had Skye tilting her head,
her dark hair falling like a curtain across her
shoulder.

'Dinner's ready.'

His voice was unrecognisable. It was so businesslike. So cold.

She turned away, rejecting him and his close-
ness, her eyes running across the golden sky, seeking warmth from its light. 'I'm not hungry.'

'I don't give a damn.'

Skye swept her eyes shut.

'You are pregnant. You must eat.'

'I'll eat when I want to. When I'm hungry.' She lifted her legs, curling them against her chest, resting her chin on her knees. She heard Matteo draw closer but didn't risk looking at him.

'Are we going to quarrel about everything?'

Skye stared straight ahead. 'I'm not quarrelling with you.'

'If that were the case you'd already be on your way downstairs for dinner.'

Skye didn't respond.

'Melania has prepared your favourite. She will be disappointed if you don't at least make an appearance.'

'That's not fair,' Skye said softly. Using her affection for his housekeeper to push her into doing what he wanted was a low trick. Then again, why would she expect him to play fair? Matteo had proven, again and again, that he would do whatever it took to get his way.

'What isn't fair?'

'You know I'd never disappoint Melania,' Skye said without meeting his eyes.

'You and she seemed to have a special bond.' Speculation stirred in the depths of his eyes.

'I guess she liked having someone in the house who wasn't a psychopath.' The insult came out on a sigh of frustration. She stood, curving her hands over the balustrade, her eyes following a gondola as it moved slowly down the canal beneath them.

Her frustration was largely aimed at herself. How had this happened? She'd come to Venice with a simple plan. And she'd been so close to freedom. If only she hadn't fainted! If only he hadn't seen!

She swept her eyes shut again, inhaling deeply. 'I'll be down soon.'

Apparently satisfied, he stalked out of the room without a backward glance, leaving Skye all alone.

CHAPTER FOUR

'DO YOU SEE these paintings, Matteo?'

Matteo's eight-year-old eyes followed the direction of his nonno's finger, nodding thoughtfully as he studied the curious artwork. 'What are they?'

Nonno's smile was rich with pride. 'They were painted by a student of Modigliani—you can see his style in the faces, no?'

Matteo nodded, though he had no idea who Modigliani was and what about the faces was reminiscent of his work. Nonetheless, he understood that the information was being imparted with gravitas and importance. He also knew that if he nodded, and at least appeared to know, it would impress his grandfather—and impressing the tall, smartly dressed man had become very important to Matteo in the six months since he'd come to live with him.

'He would spend summers here, at this very hotel, every year, and leave a painting as a gift— in lieu of payment. It is how your great-great-great-grandfather managed to collect so many of the pieces.'

'Modigliano?' Matteo prompted.

Nonno hid his smile. 'Modigliani's student,' he corrected.

'Are they valuable, Nonno?'

'Valuable, yes.' Nonno's eyes narrowed. 'But they are not for selling. They are for keeping and remembering. One day they will be yours, for you to keep and look after, and then to pass on to your son, and his son, and so forth. They are part of our family legacy, Matteo. That is their true value.'

Matteo's thirty-two-year-old eyes fell on the same painting, studying the angular face, the bright colours and the eyes that seemed to follow him about the room. Thank God his grandfather had had the foresight to strip the hotel of its artwork before the bank had claimed them as assets of the hotel and included them in the degrading fire sale.

'Ah, *signora*!' Melania's voice cracked through his reverie. He turned in time to see his wife pulled into an enormous hug by his housekeeper—a woman who had never shown him any degree of warmth or affection but apparently adored Skye. 'I'm so happy you are home!'

Skye's face drained of all colour but she covered it quickly. 'It's lovely to see you again, Melania. How have you been?'

'Busy, busy. Here, come, sit. I make you risotto.' Melania leaned closer so that Matteo had to hold his breath to hear what she said next. 'And canoli for dessert, *si*?'

'Oh, thank you.' Skye nodded, moving towards the table. Matteo watched as she pulled a seat out and arranged a napkin on her lap, all without meeting his eyes.

Her indifference infuriated him.

So too her air of cold detachment, when he knew how heated she was. He'd felt her heat— even in the hospital it had burst between them, flaring up out of nowhere. But now she had her long hair scraped back into a simple braid that ran down her back, the thick fringe sitting in silent judgement of him, and dressed in clothes that had been hers *before*. Clothes that had been left, hanging in her wardrobe, all the weeks that she had been away...

'So, Skye,' he drawled, waiting until she was settled before taking the seat opposite. He kicked back in his chair a little, his eyes unable to hide their mocking as they latched to hers. 'What exactly *was* your plan?'

She didn't pretend to misunderstand. 'It seems irrelevant now.'

His expression was unchanged. 'You were going to fly off into the Australian sunset?'

Her eyes flew to his, shock holding her body rigid. 'How did you—?'

'How did I know?' he interrupted scathingly.

'Your handbag had your ticket. So this was going to be a fly in, fly out divorce?'

She swallowed, the slender column of her throat moving visibly as she tried to keep her calm. 'Was I supposed to spend the weekend?' she fired back sarcastically, reaching for a water glass and sipping from it without shying away from his look. 'Did you want to take me sightseeing? One last ride down the Grand Canal?'

'Given that you're carrying my child, I would have expected a degree of consultation, yes. Of course, knowing your father as I do, I'm not sure why I am so surprised.'

She looked away, his statement instantly chastening her and angering her in equal measure. But she had no reason to be cowered by him. Not after what he'd done. 'That brings us to the important point, doesn't it? If you'd been honest with me from the beginning, we wouldn't be in this situation,' she pointed out.

'And because you think I lied, you felt it appropriate to repay me by keeping my child from me?' he demanded, reaching for the serving spoon and passing it to Skye.

'You did lie.' She took the implement, avoiding an accidental brush with his fingers as though they contained the plague. 'And this wasn't about repaying you.'

'No? So why not tell me about the baby?'

Skye stared at him long and hard, then shook her head. How could she answer that without admitting how much she'd loved him? Without telling her husband that his betrayal had broken her heart? Not just once, but every morning when she'd had to wake up and remember, anew, that he wasn't in bed beside her.

Pride kept her silent on that score. That he'd hurt her was bad enough—giving him the satisfaction of knowing just how badly was something she wanted to keep all to herself.

'Why not speak to me about the hotel in the first instance?' She pushed back, scooping a moderate amount of risotto onto her plate and sitting back in her chair. 'If you'd told me you wanted it, if you'd offered to buy it, I would have given that thought.'

'And you might have said no,' he responded, the words hardened by the long years he'd spent trying to get the hotel back. 'How did you learn the truth?'

'I asked our family lawyer about it,' she said quietly. 'He told me *all* about the feud with Dad. The fact you'd tried to buy the hotel. That Dad had said no. That you'd threatened to destroy him. That you'd "make him pay".' The threat sent a shiver running down Skye's spine. Marrying her would indeed have been a punishment to her father, had he lived to see it.

'That same lawyer would have stopped you from selling to me.'

Skye swallowed, silently admitting that there was truth in that. Had she not loved Matteo, would she have sold an asset to a man reputed to be ruthless and selfish just because he wanted it? Would she have sold a damned thing to someone who'd been a sworn enemy of her father? She shrugged, feigning uncertainty. 'You don't know that. I certainly didn't.'

'I knew it,' he said, the words hardened like steel.

'So, what? You decided to seduce me, to propose to me, to make me believe I was in love with you? To take my virginity? And all so you could get me to sign some stupid hotel over to you?'

He turned his face away, his profile resolute. 'The hotel that you disdain means the world to me. Losing it was not an option.'

'Oh, go to hell,' she snapped, scraping her chair back and standing jerkily. 'So that makes this okay? Me being collateral damage is something you can make your peace with because you wanted the hotel?'

He compressed his lips, studying the slender silhouette of her figure, backlit by the evening light.

'It should never have been sold. I had to return it to my family. It was my duty.'

Skye's eyes feathered closed, her lashes forming

two dark half-crescents against her cheeks. But it was confirmation—confirmation she didn't really need but somehow was useful to have. It was something to hold tight to her chest, to warn her from letting him anywhere near her heart ever again.

'It was all a lie to you. A game.' She bit down on her lip, the reality one that even now she found she couldn't quite face.

He stood and she followed his movements with eyes that were huge with her hurt.

'Not all of it.' The words were deep and sensual and should have been a warning.

But Skye was too upset to use her brain, so she glared at him angrily and prompted, 'No? You're saying you did feel *something* for me?'

'Oh yes, *cara.* I felt something for you. You cannot fake what we shared.'

And the penny dropped with insulting clarity. 'For God's sake, Matteo.' She spun away from him, moving across the room, staring out at the water beneath them. But her heart was beating at triple speed and blood gushed through her body so fast, so loudly, that she could hear its demanding torrent inside her ears.

He came to stand behind her, his words whispered into her ear. 'I hadn't expected you to be innocent.'

Skye's eyes dropped shut. That night—that

beautiful night! How tainted it was now by the knowledge she was forced to overlay on the experience. It hadn't been special and wonderful; it had been fraudulent. A deception. A lie.

'Yeah, well, I was. Innocent and stupid.'

'Why were you stupid?'

She swallowed and shook her head. But it was a mistake. He was still so close that the simple gesture brought her cheek against his chest. She moved away, a small sound of protest on her lips.

'I should have seen through you.'

Matteo didn't respond. He watched her from the small distance she'd carved out; saw the way her head was held straight, her shoulders squared, begrudgingly admiring her for the courage she demonstrated again and again.

'I'm so angry with myself. And with you!' She spun around, forgetting how close he was. But there was nowhere else for her to go—her back was against the wall, literally and figuratively. 'Did you really think I'd be so stupid in love with you, or so sex-fogged, that I'd forget to engage my brain when I signed important legal papers?' She rolled her eyes. 'I mightn't be any good at spotting cheating bastards, but I've been taught to read contracts with care before adding my signature. Even contracts prepared by my "loving" husband.' She spat the last words as a final insult. Her breath was tearing from her chest, making her whole body shift with each intake.

'But I will give you the hotel,' she said after a long, tense silence. 'I will give it to you without strings, right now. If you accept this marriage is over.'

His laugh was a dry sound. 'No.'

'You want the hotel…'

'You think I want it more than *my child*?' His eyes narrowed and there was a dangerous anger in them.

'Yes,' she said simply, her expression filled with the sadness of that truth. 'I think you are obsessed with getting the hotel back. To the exclusion of any kind of human decency or behaviour.'

His eyes darkened with intensity. 'The rules of the game have changed now.'

'Game?' she returned with undisguised fury. How could he refer to their marriage in such a cavalier fashion? She had loved him and he'd broken her heart. Anger bubbled through her.

He spoke as though she hadn't. 'My child will inherit the hotel regardless of what happens to you and me. It will be back in the Vin Santo family one way or another. That is, and always has been, my primary concern.' His eyes narrowed. 'And, in the meantime, we are married. What's yours is mine, no?'

She ground her teeth together. 'You've just got everything worked out, haven't you?'

'Not quite everything,' he said thoughtfully, taking a step towards her. A step that spoke of danger, desire and needs that had long been denied. 'I still don't know how we're going to raise a child together when we cannot be in the same room without arguing at the top of our lungs.'

Colour filled Skye's cheeks. 'I'll do whatever I need to make sure my child is happy. Even pretending to put up with you.'

His laugh sent shivers of danger dancing down her spine. 'And will you put up with this...?' he asked, taking another step towards her and brushing his lips over hers so that he felt the shiver that made her whole body tremble.

'Will you make the most of our marriage by enjoying the one thing that is good about it?' he prompted, sliding his fingers under the waistband of her shirt, connecting with the softness of her flesh.

A husky moan dropped from Skye's mouth. She closed her eyes, unwilling to see the triumph in Matteo's expression that she knew would be there. If she were to admit how badly she wanted this, and him, he would have every right to gloat.

How could she still desire him, even after what

he'd done? He'd proven himself to be the worst kind of bastard, yet her body, her treacherous, hungry, body was his for a song.

'No,' she heard herself say, and practically groaned at the word. 'And I know you won't force me.'

He froze, every line in his body like iron. 'Force you? *Dio!*' He stepped back and it was as though ice water had doused them both. 'Of course I am not going to *force* you. What the hell do you think I am? A savage?'

She tried to summon her anger. To rally it to her defence. But there was only sadness now. Grief and despondence at how much she had lost—and the minefield that lay before them.

'I think you're a horrible person,' she said softly. 'I think you're capable of anything. And I hate you.'

'You think I'd force you into my bed?'

'You've forced me into this marriage,' she whispered. 'How is it any different?'

He spun away from her, stalking to the table and sipping his wine. She could see from the set of his shoulders, the straightness of his spine, that she had upset him. Good. Let him feel some of the darkness she was contending with.

'You married me of your own free will,' he said, without turning to face her. 'You chose this life. I am simply holding you to that commitment.'

His logic was both undeniable and astounding all at once. 'I chose a life that was based on lies...'

'Yes, yes, so you've said. But when did I lie?' He spun around, his eyes pinning her to the spot, his question raking her heart over steaming hot coals.

'The whole time! You...'

'Yes?' he prompted. 'What did I say to you that wasn't true?'

Skye opened her mouth, staring at her husband, her mind drawing an absolute blank. 'It was nothing you said, not specifically. It was *everything* you pretended to be.'

'And what was that?'

'Someone who loved me.' She whispered the words, the hurt in her heart a weight she couldn't dispense with. She was glad, in that moment, that she'd never told him the true grief of her upbringing, the loneliness that had lived inside her for as long as she could recall. A loneliness borne of being utterly unloved and unwanted that had only finally eased when she'd met Matteo.

For the first time in her life she'd felt special. Cossetted. Adored. Wanted for who she was, for all of herself.

What an easy target she'd been for him!

'Did I say that?' he queried, the words a simple

question. He could have no concept of how cutting they were. Of how cold and cruel.

Skye nodded, but her mouth drew downwards.

Had he ever said those three little words? She had said them often, so often, and she had meant them each time. Had she thought she could love him enough for both of them? Had she thought it would mean something if she kept saying it? That it would make it true and right?

'No.' She whispered the word, grief bringing the sting of tears to her throat. 'You never said it. But you must have known that I just presumed… that I thought you loved me.'

'Love is irrelevant,' he snapped impatiently. He'd been in love before and he hadn't enjoyed the experience one bit.

'Not to me! Loving you, wanting you, it was all tied up in one for me.'

He prowled closer, his eyes holding hers. He stopped right in front of her, so close that she could feel the warmth emanating from his body—a warmth that was at complete odds with the coldness of his heart. 'There is no love here, *cara*. It is best that you accept that and take what I'm willing to offer.'

'And what's that?' she muttered, her heart cracking irreparably.

'A place in my bed. And a promise to pleasure you in all the ways I know you love…'

* * *

Matteo's words, his stunningly arrogant 'offer', stayed lodged in Skye's head, chasing itself around, burning through her blood, making her body super-charged with a desire that she resented fully.

The problem was that he had always been an incredible lover. Of course, she had no other point of reference, but she'd always found herself tipping over the edge of pleasure, time and time again. He had learned her body's ways so quickly, supplicating her to him with insulting ease. He had been able to touch her breasts and bring her to orgasm; he had kissed her most private, sensitive parts and she'd fallen apart, piece by piece, until she was broken and rebuilt in an image of passion and need.

He had woken her by moving over her, pushing inside her, stirring her to wakefulness from within, his body commanding hers effortlessly. He'd taught her so much about desire, need and sensual heat.

He had been gentle when she'd needed it, and demanding and firm in a way that had raised every single goose-bump on her body. He had kissed every square inch of her flesh, branding himself on her in a million different ways.

And she had always wanted him.

But now, with her hormones in a state of rampant disarray, desire was thick in her veins, threatening to weaken her.

Worse, threatening to lead her to him.

Skye flipped over in the bed, staring at the wall across the room with its ornate wallpaper that she could just make out in the moonlit darkness of the room.

Tears that she'd held at bay all night were closer to the surface now, wetting her eyes and thickening her throat. The wall grew fuzzy before her eyes as grief enveloped her. She pressed a hand to her stomach, breathing deeply, imagining their baby inside her.

How she'd wanted this pregnancy! For the most part, they'd taken precautions, but not every time. And, on those occasions, Skye had wanted a baby to be the result more than she could ever have said.

And she'd got her wish, only the joy she'd anticipated was nowhere to be seen.

The discovery, after leaving Matteo, that they'd created a baby together had presented a whole new world of problems. For, almost immediately after, reality had descended on her like a hurricane. It might have taken two of them to create a baby, but there wouldn't be two of them raising it.

She'd be alone.

Again.

Like always.

Yet not alone, because there would be a baby

him to weave. He had lied to her but, oh, she'd been begging for the lie.

For the love.

She'd been so desperate for anyone to love her that she hadn't stopped for a moment to question a single, damned thing. She'd learned, years earlier, that fairy tales didn't exist...so why had she let herself forget that so easily?

to care for. A baby she would love with all her heart. She'd love it enough for both of them, and she'd make sure the baby grew up to be kind and smart, adored and loved.

And her child would never be capable of acting like Matteo had!

Skye was determined that she would do everything right and give the baby all the love she'd never known. As well as stability and adoration, support and acceptance. She'd only known the baby to be inside her for days before she'd begun to make wholesale changes to her life and lifestyle.

She didn't want to raise her child as the heir or heiress to a billion-pound fortune—let alone two! She didn't want them to equate wealth with luck or success. While she wanted her child to have everything it needed in life, Skye knew first-hand that true needs weren't based on financial wealth. Not beyond the immediate concerns, in any event. A roof over one's head, a bed, enough food not to feel hungry… Once these things were taken care of, what more did one need?

She'd always had more than she needed, materially. But when it came to love?

She had been starved in the cruellest of ways.

A tear slid out of one eye, landing with a thud onto the silk pillow beneath her.

She'd been such a perfect target for Matteo's plans—what an easy deception it had been for

CHAPTER FIVE

Two years earlier

HE WAS, WITHOUT a doubt, the most stunning man Skye had ever seen. Her eyes kept seeking him out, even when she knew she should have been paying better attention to the people she was locked in conversation with. After all, this party was for her family's charity, and she was the sole surviving member of the Johnson fortune.

How their ranks had dwindled! From her great-grandfather who'd had six children, to her grandfather who had raised four, and then to her father, who had come along with his inability to commit, his incessant cheating, his determination not to settle.

Skye had been the result of an affair with an air hostess and, had her grandfather never intervened, she doubted her father would have known she existed, far less taken an interest in her upbringing.

She had cousins, of course. But, while they'd inherited million-pound fortunes, it was Skye alone who'd been left the reins of the business empire.

Undoubtedly because no one had realised how

quickly her father would die—his skiing accident had been a completely unexpected death. Weeks later, her grandfather had died. The rumours spoke of a broken heart—but Skye suspected it had more to do with his daily habit of over-indulgence in whisky.

She'd become a billion-pound heiress at nine years of age, and a childhood always marred by neglect and disinterest had descended into a barren wasteland devoid of human contact. Boarding school, where she'd found it hard to fit in; a great-aunt who'd tolerated Skye for the briefest stints possible during school holidays, and generally only when a nanny couldn't be found to care for her.

Her eyes flicked sideways and landed straight on his face. He was watching her. A *frisson* of something new and intriguing glanced across her spine.

'We're on track to open the children's hospice by Christmas,' the charity's chairman Mr Wu said, his round face beaming.

'That's very good.' Skye nodded. Generally, she was passionate about the children's foundation. It had been one of the initiatives she'd launched when she'd turned twenty-one and had taken control of her family's assets. It was then that she'd begun to attend the board meetings—despite her CEO's misgivings. Gradually, she'd taken more and more of an interest in the running of the business, and had even planned to enrol in law school at some point to augment the corporate education she was gaining through her involvement with the company. The children's work had long been at the fore of her mind, yet she found it almost impossible to focus on the discussions in that moment.

His eyes were so dark they were like granite. She'd never seen anything quite like it. His dark hair, thick and raven's black, was brushed back from her brow, and his face was strong and angular. Handsome? She couldn't have said. Striking, definitely, and utterly breath-taking. It wasn't that he was good-looking as much as he had an indefinable appeal. An attraction that slammed into her from the other side of the room.

Then, there was his body. Broad-shouldered, tall, he looked like an ancient warrior. She could easily imagine him in metal armour, running into battle, his autocratic face determined, his mouth set in a grim line of reckoning.

A shiver ran all the way down her spine and her nipples peaked against the gauze fabric of her gown.

Her cheeks had a guilty, self-conscious flush as she trained her attention back on Mr Wu, listening with determination now, forcing herself to nod and comprehend even when her brain was trying to record if his hands were as large and dominant as the rest of his body. More so, had he been wearing a wedding ring?

The thought came to her out of nowhere. Her blush deepened. Her temperature was skyrocketing—she felt as though she could spontaneously combust at a moment's notice.

Mr Wu made a joke and she laughed, but she couldn't have repeated it for a billion pounds.

It was at least an hour later—an hour filled with meaningless chit chat and forced laughter, an hour in which her eyes had mercilessly followed his progress around the room—when Skye finally found herself face to face with him.

The man who had become rapidly an absolute obsession for her.

'We meet at last.' His voice was better than she could have imagined. The words were husky, thick with a foreign accent. Italian? Greek?

Whatever, they sounded like sunshine and seduction and drove everything but desire from her mind. Skye's lips parted, her eyes flew wide and her mouth was dry—her tongue too thick possibly to admit speech.

It was a completely unfamiliar impulse, but her fingertips tingled with a desire to lift to his chest; to touch him for herself.

Perhaps he felt the same thing because his hand caught hers and lifted it to his lips.

'I'm Matteo Vin Santo,' he said, his eyes probing hers, waiting for a reaction.

There was none—not one of recognition anyway. Skye's father had died before he could tell her the whole sordid history with the Vin Santos, and her grandfather so soon afterwards. Who would have enlightened her about their ancient grudge?

Nobody.

So Skye smiled, a smile of pure, innocent curiosity. A smile that was like a lamb willingly heading towards its own slaughter.

'Skye Johnson.'

'I know.' His wink was slow and deliberate; its effect was marked. Her stomach swooped with instant awareness.

'My reputation precedes me, huh?'

'The place has your name on the door.' His grin was devilish.

'Sorry about that. They insisted.'

'They tend to do that when you donate millions of pounds.' Another wink. Skye's whole body winked back. She felt her insides squeeze with needs she'd never known she possessed and her heart rolled in her chest.

'Ah. Occupational hazard, then,' she managed to murmur, surprised that she could sound normal and calm when her chest was hammering with the force of a very localised typhoon.

'The cost of philanthropy.' His eyes roamed her

face thoughtfully, and Skye felt as though he was seeing all manner of secrets and thoughts. All of the things she usually kept wrapped up, tight in her chest.

And she didn't even mind.

'I suppose I'll learn to live with it.' She smiled at him. He smiled back. Her heart clicked into a new gear.

'You know, it's all very refined and elegant,' he said, with obvious disapproval despite the compliment. 'But I'd kill for an actual meal. I don't suppose you'd join me for dinner, Skye Johnson?'

Skye blinked, her expression clouding with doubts for the briefest of moments, and then she nodded. 'I suppose I would,' she murmured, not even questioning the familiarity when he reached down and laced his fingers through hers.

'Let's go, then.'

Perhaps it was her broken sleep the night before. The dreams that had tormented her, shaking her whenever she'd felt close to sleep. Perhaps it was the memories that those dreams had invoked, little shards of the past that had dug painfully into her sides all night, reminding her of what a fool she'd been.

Perhaps it was the way her heart had been tripping back into love in her sleep, against her wishes, reminding her of how she'd felt when first they'd met. Of the way he'd smiled and she'd answered. Of how simple it had all seemed, and of how right it had felt.

Whatever the reason, the second Skye laid eyes on Matteo the next morning she felt as if she'd been pounded by a sledge hammer. He was dressed in a navy-blue suit with a crisp white shirt open at the neck to reveal the thick column of his neck, the dark hairs curling at the base. She had to pause just inside the kitchen door—to brace herself physically before moving deeper into his atmosphere.

How absurd. There was no such thing as 'his' atmosphere. There was only air, and it belonged equally to both of them. Never mind that he changed the feeling of everything simply by being in it—simply by existing.

His eyes lifted to hers, roaming her face, seeing everything she wanted to keep hidden, just as he had that first night they'd met. No doubt he saw the bags under her eyes and the pallor of her skin.

Good.

Let him see how miserable she was!

Let him feel some of the blame for his hand in that. Except he wasn't capable of such an emotion, was he? Since she'd returned to Venice, he'd been unremorseful and unapologetic.

'I wasn't sure what you are eating,' he said conversationally, as though there was nothing awkward about being back in his home more than a month after she'd left, presuming she'd seen the last of him and it for ever. 'I had Melania prepare an assortment of things.' He nodded towards the platter in the centre of the table. Skye's attention drifted to it and her stomach gave a little lurch of nausea.

'Just coffee,' she said, hoping she wasn't about to experience her first bout of morning sickness and vomit all over the tiled floor. Then again, she might get his expensive designer shoes in the process, so there would be some consolation...

'Are you able to drink coffee in your condition?'

Skye's nod was terse. 'A cup a day is fine,' she said. 'Far more risk if I don't have it.'

'To the baby?' he enquired with interest.

'To whomever denies me.' The words were delivered without a hint of humour yet Matteo smiled, dipping his head forward so that she saw only the quickest flicker of amusement on his face before he stood and moved into the kitchen area.

She watched as he retrieved the pot, pouring a good measure into one of the mugs and carrying it over to her. His eyes held hers as he passed it forward but this time, when she tried to carefully manoeuvre her fingers so that she avoided any skin-to-skin contact, he made it impossible.

He placed a hand over hers, curving her fingers around the edge of the coffee cup, his eyes locked to hers in a way that made breathing hurt.

'How did you sleep?' The question was asked with a raw intensity. She ignored it, refusing to buy into the cessation of hostilities.

She'd been manipulated by him once before—she was just going to have to work extra hard to avoid it happening again.

'Fine, thank you.'

'I wish I could say the same,' he muttered.

'Bad dreams?' she responded archly.

'Very, very good dreams,' he corrected, the words silky, his implication clear. Still, he added, 'Memories.'

'Ah.' She cleared her throat and took a step away, retrieving her hand still wrapped around the coffee cup, and telling herself that the warmth spreading through her body had to do with the lure of caffeine rather than anything more threatening to her equilibrium.

She lifted the mug upwards, breathing in its tantalising aroma, and fierce, beautiful memories slashed through her. How many coffees had they shared?

Though their marriage had been short, coffee had been a lifeblood of it, and they'd indulged their mutual obsession often. Side by side and, she had thought at the time, in complete harmony.

Physically, emotionally and intellectually. How wrong she'd been.

The thoughts weren't helpful. She pushed them aside angrily.

'I have to go into the office today. Just for a few hours.'

Skye didn't turn around. It was a heck of a lot easier to think when she wasn't looking at him. The memories were less forceful. 'Fine,' she said with a nod. 'Why are you telling me?'

Silence.

'I mean, it's not like before, is it?' she asked, the words soft. 'I have no expectation you'll change your schedule for me. In fact, I'd really prefer you wouldn't.'

'It's not like before,' he agreed, coming to stand beside her. 'You are pregnant. The idea of leaving you alone doesn't sit well with me.'

Skye rolled her eyes. 'I'm growing a baby. It's not a particularly high-risk activity.'

'You fell into the canal yesterday,' he reminded her. Unnecessarily. It had taken four showers to wash the smell of Venice out of her hair.

'And I'm still here today,' she said with a shrug. She sipped the coffee, closing her eyes in appreciation as it made its way into her body.

'Does it happen often?'

She shook her head. 'Fainting? That was the fourth time.'

'Why?'

'It's a blood pressure thing,' Skye said, trying to remember the specifics. 'Some women are more prone to it than others. One minute I'm fine, and then I'm all faint, and there are stars in my eyes and the ground rushes up towards me.'

He didn't say anything, which Skye took to mean the conversation was closed. Good. She smiled in his general direction. 'I might drink my coffee in my room,' she said, needing space from him. Distance. Time.

'Aspetti,' he said. 'Wait a moment.' His accent was thicker once more, husky and dark.

She paused, not looking at him. 'Yes?'

'I don't like this.' She heard the frown in his voice. 'I will change my plans. You clearly shouldn't be left alone.'

Panic raced through Skye. 'I'm *fine*!' She spun around to face him, and one look at his expression made her stomach drop. His expression was as determined as she'd ever seen it.

Great.

'Melania is here,' Skye pointed out desperately.

'She has enough to do without playing nurse-maid to you.'

'And you don't?' Skye retorted quickly. 'When we were together you were gone twelve hours a day.'

'And you missed me,' he said smoothly.

She rolled her eyes. 'That's not the point I'm making. I only mean that I'm used to you not being here.'

He moved closer. 'It is my baby. And you are my wife. That makes this my responsibility.'

Responsibility. Pain washed over Skye. How long had she felt like a burden? Like she was someone's responsibility and never their joy? How long had she known herself to be cared for out of duty rather than love? The idea that he might be doing so now was galling. And many other things!

She swallowed, but the razor blades in her throat didn't abate.

'You have too much to do. Melania can easily call you if there's a problem.'

'This is not a negotiation,' he said with the ruthless determination she'd come to expect from him. 'I've made up my mind.'

Skye clamped her teeth together, grinding them out of frustration. He obviously wasn't going to listen to reason, but maybe she could use his concern for the baby to get her own way.

'You want to do the right thing? Then go to work. Being around you is definitely no good for my blood pressure.'

He arched a brow and his lips lifted in the hint of a smile. 'I imagine I elevate your blood pressure,' he said silkily. 'And fainting is usually associated with low blood pressure, is it not? So perhaps having me here is going to be just the medicine you need.'

Skye shook her head, but Matteo moved to the table, holding a chair out.

'Sit down, Skye. You're not going to win this, so you might as well save your breath to argue about something that matters.'

'You don't think my personal freedom matters?' she snapped, staying right where she was.

'I think the baby's safety is our number one priority.'

Chastened, she dipped her head forward. 'I'll be fine.'

'Yes. And I will be here to make sure of it.'

He took his seat at the table and returned his attention to the newspaper, flicking straight to the finance section.

Skye expelled a soft sigh. It was a big house. The fact that he was going to be somewhere in it didn't mean that they'd be falling all over each other. She'd just make a point of staying in her room, or on the rooftop terrace—places where he wouldn't be.

'Okay, whatever.' She shrugged. 'Just remember, there's many months of this to go. That's a long time for you to be out of the office.'

His shrug was pure, sexy indolence. 'I'll be cutting my hours back once the baby is born anyway, so why not start now?'

'Why would you?' Skye demanded, appalled.

'You don't think I will want to spend time with our child? You don't think his or her birth warrants my being here?'

'No!' Too desperate. Too urgent. 'Matteo, this is *my* baby! You agreed to divorce me yesterday. And now you're acting as if we're going to spend every spare moment together for the next eighteen years.'

'At least,' he remarked, his expression droll.

At Skye's obvious panic, he issued a somewhat placatory smile. 'Skye, I had no idea you were pregnant when you came to obtain my signature, as you very well know. Surely you can see that it changes everything?'

'Not for me,' she pointed out caustically. 'I have as little desire to be married to you now as I did then.'

'And I have as much conviction that you are lying now as I did then.'

'Why do you find it so hard to believe that a woman wouldn't want to be married to you? Are you that arrogant, Matteo? Do you really think that after everything you did I'd want to be your wife?'

He sat back in his chair, his eyes resting on her face with curiosity. 'And what did I do?'

Skye's laugh was a hollow intonation. 'Seriously? You want me to catalogue your faults? You've already admitted them.'

A muscle jerked in his jaw. 'I wanted the hotel,' he said with a shrug. 'It changed nothing about our marriage. Nothing about how you felt for me.'

'It changed *everything*! My God, Matteo! You targeted me! I had *no* idea who you were that night but you knew everything about me. I didn't even know about your feud with my family until a little over a month ago. But you did. You knew all about it! You flirted with me and you seduced me, yet it had *nothing* to do with who I am, right? It was all a fake!'

'The passion was not.'

Though it was such a meagre compliment, a tiny crumb of assurance, Skye shook her head dismissively. 'Would you have felt the same way if there was no hotel? Would you have asked me to marry you?'

His eyes gave nothing away. He was all ruthless, dynamic tycoon. The breakfast table might as well have been in a boardroom, for how comfortable he looked behind it.

'What do you want me to say, Skye? We have discussed this. I married you for the hotel. I wish it hadn't been necessary. But this does not mean there weren't certain…benefits to our marriage.'

She dropped her jaw, her eyes clashing with

his ruthless gaze. 'I truly can't believe you would stoop so low!'

'I used what means were necessary.' He shrugged his shoulders with apparent unconcern. 'You were all too eager to merge our assets. To give me open slather of your portfolio. That was not my decision, but yours.'

'Yes,' she agreed softly. 'But only because I was in love with you. And I thought you loved me back! Only because I thought our marriage was genuine and your affections were true. If I'd known that the assets were the sole reason you'd proposed then believe me, Matteo, I would have fought you every step of the way.'

'Which is precisely why I had to marry you.' The words were softly voiced.

He stood abruptly, moving around the table. He stopped beside her and crouched down on his powerful haunches so that the fabric of his pants pulled across his strong thighs. She forced herself to look away, but not before the effect of his nearness had imprinted on her consciousness, reminding her of how she had felt pinned beneath those legs, pinned beneath him.

Her mouth was dry, her temperature skyrocketing.

He lifted his fingers to her chin and forced her face back to his, lifting it up so that their faces were level.

'This conversation is redundant. It changes nothing about what we both want now.'

His lips crushed down on hers, shocking her at the same time it answered every single ache that was ripping through her. She surrendered to his kiss even when she knew she ought to fight him. To fight their attraction.

But she was selfish, she was hungry and she had been denied his touch for so long. She needed his touch. It was on the tip of her tongue to whisper the word that was chasing round and round in her mind—*please*—but out of nowhere his words bubbled through her.

'You'll be begging me to take you in no time. And I'm going to enjoy it, Mrs Vin Santo.'

So she said nothing. She kissed him, because she wasn't strong enough not to, but she didn't beg, even when her heart was doing just that.

CHAPTER SIX

SKYE FLIPPED ONTO her back and listened to her meditation even harder, concentrating so much on being relaxed that she became even more agitated when sleep didn't come. And, the more she concentrated on needing to sleep, the harder it became to make peace with the fact that she was still awake, so that she clicked the recording right back to the beginning and focused even harder.

To no avail.

After an hour of breathing deeply, and picturing a still ocean with a single ray of light shimmering across its surface, she was agitated and cranky.

She reached for her phone, silenced the patronising recording and checked the time.

It was just after midnight, and she was wide awake.

With a rustle of the silk sheets, she slipped out of bed, padding across the bedroom to the window. Ancient timber shutters blocked out the noise and lights of Venice. She pushed them outwards—they groaned a little in complaint before opening wide. Just beneath the window was a planter box overflowing with bright red geraniums. They were on almost every window sill in Matteo's villa—though some boasted lavender as well. The fragrance was heady, especially in the spring when an army of bees would swarm across the blossoms, picking them over for sustenance.

Skye reached down and plucked a geranium stalk, twirling it around and then bringing it to her nose. There was an almost metallic fragrance that brought back such memories of her first few weeks in Italy, when she'd picked small bunches and placed them on either side of their bed so that they were the second thing she saw each morning—after Matteo.

He'd teased her for doing it. 'Melania can get you anything you want from the market, you know. Much prettier flowers that will make much bigger arrangements.'

'I like these,' she had insisted with a shrug. 'They're bright and sunny and they grow right outside the window. They're our flowers.'

She had, at the time, liked the way that had sounded. *Ours.* As though the stupid word could infer a degree of seriousness on them that hadn't actually existed.

She tossed the bloom carelessly from the window, leaning forward by a small degree to watch its progress. The air offered little resistance to such a robust bloom. It dragged quickly to the ground, dropping with a soft *thunk* into the water below. It hovered on the surface for a moment, as though looking at her accusingly, before falling further, dropping downwards and disappearing for good.

Even the most beautiful things met their end eventually.

Their marriage should have been one of them.

Their marriage should never have happened, she corrected herself inwardly. That damned hotel! It was one of many properties owned by her family trust. If he hadn't made such an obvious effort to move it to his own possession, she wouldn't have particularly known it existed.

Was there any excuse that could justify what he'd done? Marrying to secure a piece of property?

Sleeping with her—being her first lover as well as her first love?

Could she ever forgive him that duplicity? Did she dare even try?

A warm breeze rustled in the open windows. She angled her face upwards, giving the air full access to her front, letting it loosen her hair, pulling it back from her face. And she breathed in deeply. Geraniums, people, ice-cream, Venice… It was all so familiar.

Her restlessness grew.

She pressed her fingers to her tummy, thinking of their baby. 'Is this your doing?' she whispered. 'Are you making Mummy wake up when it's time to sleep?'

She'd read a book on pregnancy, cover to cover, when she'd first learned of her condition, and it had spoken of pregnancy insomnia—a hormonal condition, not related to the size of the baby so much as the fact it was there, super-charging a woman's blood and body so that sleep became chemically impossible.

She told herself that was the culprit even when she knew, deep down, that it had so much more to do with Matteo's kiss. She sucked in a breath, lifting her fingers to her lips and touching the trembling flesh there.

It had been over in a moment. Just a quick reminder of how he could reduce her to ash and smoke with no effort at all. He had stood afterwards, apparently completely unaffected, and he'd left her alone to eat. To brood. To stew.

And, despite the fact he'd changed his schedule so that he could keep an eye on her throughout the day, she'd barely seen him. He'd been close by at all times, but not in her space.

A fact she should have appreciated...but didn't.

The kiss had stirred something up inside her.

A desire that she had presumed had died with their marriage. A desire that was unwelcome, unwanted and utterly confusing.

Another warm breeze ran across her flesh, spreading goose-bumps with it.

Sleep seemed impossible to grasp and attempting to do so made no sense. On the spur of the moment, she moved across her room quietly, pulling the door inward gently. She paused, listening for a moment. The house was quiet. Was he asleep?

The image was striking.

He slept naked.

Always naked.

Her heart throbbed inside her chest as her eyes ran down the hallway towards his bedroom—the bedroom they'd shared.

Was he in there now, naked, tanned, virile…? Was he in there, thinking about her?

She forced herself to look away. She had no intention of giving in to her body's physical needs. She wasn't that stupid, or that weak.

She turned in the opposite direction and made her way along the corridor, her eyes skimming over the impressive collection of art—some of it Renaissance, much of it more modern—until she reached the wide stairs inlaid with mosaics. They were as they'd been when the home had first been built, and Skye had always felt a little disrespectful when she'd walked on the practical artwork. She moved upwards with care to the next level of the house, which boasted guest rooms and an impressive library, not stopping to remove a book from the shelves that she'd come to love.

When she'd first arrived in Venice, a newly-wed who'd believed that all the happiness of the world was before her, she'd decided she'd read her way through the books, starting at the top left and moving all the way across, then sliding down a shelf. She'd decided that it didn't matter what she read—history, romance, fiction, non-fiction—they were all stories and she was hungry for them to become a part of her.

She'd read sixteen books. She remembered quite clearly where she was up to on the shelf. She'd had the last book in her handbag the day she'd gone to Matteo's office. The day she'd read the contracts and started to wonder at the phrasing. The day the penny had finally started to drop.

She'd never finished the story and didn't plan to.

With a determined tilt of her chin, she moved upwards. The staircase narrowed once she turned the corner, and a small window let in a sharp blade of moonlight. She skipped past it quickly, almost surprised that it didn't slice through her with its bright intensity. At the top of the stairs, a narrow door stood closed. She rested her palm against it for a second, steeling herself for what she knew lay beyond.

Even on this side, at the top of the ancient stair-case surrounded by darkness, she could picture the rooftop garden. The bougainvillea that seemed to have a life all of its own, clambering across the timber beams, forming a sort of green room. It would be covered in an extravagant blanket of purple flowers, so vibrant that they had always reminded Skye of plums cast from paper. But the bougainvillea didn't have full autonomy amongst the scrambling vines. There was wisteria too, fragrant and heavy with the grape-shaped blooms. They were disarray in the midst of order, greenery and earth in a city shaped by the sea. She had loved the juxtaposition of their wildness against the plain blue sky. She had sat beneath them, reading, sipping iced tea and dreaming of Matteo, feeling the sun on her legs as though it were his hands or his mouth.

There was the plunge pool, tiled and neat, with views over the ocean towards the mainland. She had dipped her body into it whenever the heat had become too much, refreshing herself in its soothing water, propped against the pool coping and staring at the view with a deep sense of gratitude and a very full heart.

It was here that they'd first made love, and it was impossible not to carry that memory with her as she finally pushed the door open and moved onto the terrace. The night had been so perfect; every time she'd been on the terrace its memory had wrapped around her, filling her with a sense of complete disbelief. How had she been so lucky? To have met and fallen in love with a man like Matteo—it was more than she'd ever believed possible. And that had been a good way to feel. It wasn't possible. His love had been a fraud. A fake.

The terrace was dimly lit—only a single lamp now illuminating the ghostly outline of her favourite vines, giving them an ethereal, slightly eerie feel. The stars shone as though heaven had been blanketed by diamonds and there was a splashing noise that drew her reluctant gaze.

Reluctant, because she knew immediately who was creating the noise.

Who else could it be?

This was Matteo's private sanctuary, where he came to escape the hectic speed of the real world. And he'd let her, and no one else, in to enjoy it. At the time, that had flattered her. Now? It was a very cheap price to pay for the hotel he had hoped to steal.

Colour danced along her cheek bones. Angry colour.

How dared he be so beautiful? The moon seemed to caress his flesh, spreading diamond dust over his shoulders and back as he stared out at the view she had loved so much. Droplets of water shivered from his dark pelt of hair, glancing his broad shoulders before slipping lower, over his arms.

Desire swirled in her gut.

Skye ignored it.

This had been a bad idea. A stupid, stupid thought. She took a step backwards, moving towards the open door, needing to put all the distance she could between herself and her husband.

She didn't want to speak to him. She couldn't see any *more* of him. Was he wearing bathers? Or swimming naked, as they'd always done in the past?

A husk of breath caught in her throat and she spun, needing distance.

Splashing.

And then his voice, low and commanding. 'Skye.'

She froze, her eyes shut, her lips parted.

Her pulse was a raging torrent of need. Damn it! Why did she feel this for him even when she hated him for what he'd done?

'Turn around.' The words were a command and she wanted to ignore them. She hardened her heart to the power he had over her, or tried to at least. She wanted to run. She wanted to ignore him, to pretend she hadn't heard. But it was obvious she had, and the idea of seeming afraid of him in any way was anathema to Skye.

She turned slowly. She looked around with great care, as one might lift one's eyes to study a solar eclipse, expecting at any moment to be burned by the sight of him.

Only it was less a solar eclipse and more a moonlit fairy tale. The beam of light bounced off him and wisped like a cloud between them, drawing her in, pulling at her as gravity might, if it were silvery and glittered.

She swallowed, taking a step forward without realising it.

He walked through the water in time with her own steps, so that he reached the edge nearest to her at the same time Skye's toes met the grouting. His powerful body ripped him from the water with ease; the water droplets scattered over his flesh, pulling her gaze downward to the chaotic wetness that moved over his chest.

'I couldn't sleep,' she explained, her eyes locked with his even when she knew she needed to look away. The air around them was thick, and it had more to do with their past, their present, than the heat of the balmy summer night.

No, it was the whisperings of their story that was wrapping around them, pulling them back in, and for Skye's part all she could see was the never-ending nature of it all. The love she'd felt for him had turned to hate, but there was still so much love there too. For, having never loved before, not properly, she had given her love to Matteo with no expectation or hope of return.

She had given him her heart for life, and there was no way to take it back.

Despite what he'd done.

And now? A baby that would bind them for ever; the future yawned before her like a mine-field of needs she would have to navigate.

She had to do it better.

She had to draw a line in the sand and keep him firmly on one side of it.

But she also needed him. His mouth, his hands, his body.

All of him.

Need was all she could hear, and it was torment-ing her with the loudness of its demands and the insistence that she indulge it.

With the last shred of will-power she possessed, she smiled—a smile that was sense and reason in the midst of their moonshine madness. 'Are you done?' she asked, unknowingly caustic. 'I thought I'd go for a swim.'

His fingers reached for her, and the second they connected with her she drew a sharp gasp of breath. It didn't help.

'In this?' he asked, reaching for her cotton nightgown, the teasing smile on his lips sucking her further back into the vortex of their past, to a time when that smile had driven her wild. When it had made her feel connected to him and full of pleasure—not just sexual pleasure, but true pleasure at the place she had in his life, and the place he had in hers.

That smile was a dangerous lie. Listening to it would be foolish. And she was no longer foolish. At least, she was no longer so easy to fool.

'No.' A whisper.

'May I?' He held the fabric in his fingers—she held her breath in her lungs. His meaning was impossible to misinterpret.

Knowing she was playing with fire, that they were on the precipice of a very, very steep ravine, that she was one crazy decision away from falling head-first into it, she nonetheless nodded. Her eyes latched to his as he lifted, so slowly that impatience ran through her, guiding the fabric along her body, brushing it over her flesh as he balled it at her waist, pausing there, his knuckles glancing across her skin. Higher still, he teased the sensitive flesh at the side of her breasts so that she bit down on her lower lip, wondering if he'd touch her and what she'd say if he did.

'Hands up,' he said with a smile that sunk her stomach.

She complied readily, her eyes still clinging to his, as if held there by an invisible magnetic force. She reached for the heavens and he lifted the fabric the rest of the way, leaving her standing before him in just a simple lace thong.

He tossed the fabric aside carelessly, hooking

it onto the edge of a sunbed before returning his full attention to Skye.

The moon slid silver across her flesh, across his face, bathing them in the magic of that moment.

'May I?' The same question, but his voice was deeper, huskier, and she wasn't sure what he intended.

She nodded anyway, watching as he pressed his palms to her stomach first, his fingers splayed wide, as if looking for proof of the pregnancy in her abdomen. As if seeking confirmation, his eyes found hers, and she felt the swirl of emotion between them—the hunger, the need, the anger, the betrayal. It was all around her, making it impossible for Skye to know what she felt and what she wanted. Only she knew she shouldn't want this. That she should put an end to what was happening.

His hands moved higher, cupping her breasts, running over her nipples. It was an achingly familiar touch. Though it had been more than a month since she'd been naked with him, she had never forgotten the perfection of this.

It was hard to forget when memories haunted your dreams.

'I want to kiss you,' he murmured, moving his hands back to her hips, holding her still, needing her as much as she needed him. He was wet, his body slick with the pool water. Skye's eyes dropped to his chest. His heart was in there.

The heart that was cold and ruthless and hurtful. The heart she would never hold in her hands, as he held hers in his. She swallowed, danger swirling around her.

Could she sleep with him anyway?

Could she fall back into his bed, knowing that he didn't love her?

Whenever they'd been together in the past she'd truly believed that they'd been making love. That their desire was a physical representation of their emotional commitment. But Matteo had never loved her. She doubted he was even capable of the emotion.

Could she ignore that fact? Could she let sex slowly ease that pain? Wasn't it better than nothing?

'What's stopping you?' she asked softly. But the words were rich with her doubt and uncertainty.

Matteo lifted his thumb, padding it over her lip. 'What do you want?'

Skye's smile was a pale imitation of the real deal. 'You didn't care what I wanted this morning.'

'You wanted me to kiss you then.'

Skye blinked, looking away, swallowing, trying to untangle the knot of her desire and thoughts.

'And now?' she prompted.

His smile was loaded with self-deprecation. 'I

can't hear what you want over what I want. I need you to tell me.'

She sliced her eyes back to his face, her breath forced as she struggled to take stock of that moment. 'What do *you* want?' she asked with a quiet intensity.

His face cracked with an unfamiliar emotion. 'I want it to be like it used to be.'

Surprise spread through her, until she realised he was just talking about sex. Again. He wanted her whenever need overtook him. He wanted her willing, compliant body at his command.

Her response was throaty. 'It's not possible.'

He looked as though he was about to say something, but apparently changed his mind. 'Swim with me.'

It wasn't an invitation; it wasn't a command. It was simply an idea, one that moved through her. They'd swum together so often in the past. Was there anything wrong with doing so one last time?

She nodded jerkily, moving closer to the water's edge. Skye dove in with an unconscious grace. The pool wasn't long, only ten metres, but it was very deep. She had always enjoyed trying to swim down and touch the bottom, dragging her fingertips over the smooth tiles, tracing the lines of grout, holding her breath until she'd felt like her lungs might burst. She did so now, gliding right to the base, where it was dark and quiet, and she felt the bottom like it was a touchstone that could take her back.

A touchstone that had the power of rewind. That could slide her through the veils of time into the past. The past where she'd been happy—where she'd believed their marriage to be real.

But it was temporary.

She emerged in the present, the same uncertainty clogging between them, and made her way to the pool edge that overlooked the ocean. It was dark now, only a few cruise ships visible, their bright lights showing the outline of the boats. Matteo swam beside her, bracing himself against the pool, his elbow lightly brushing hers.

Skye didn't move away.

'I've been wondering something,' he said, not looking in her direction.

'Yeah?'

'When did you find out?'

She tilted her head towards his slowly, her eyes running over his autocratic profile, noting the details of his features even as she tried to make sense of the question.

'About the baby,' he clarified, the words deep and husky.

'Oh.' She looked away again. Her face was pale beneath the moon's light. 'A couple of weeks ago.'

He was quiet for a long moment. So long that

she wondered if perhaps he hadn't heard or hadn't understood.

'And how did you feel?'

'How did I feel?' she repeated, a frown spreading across her face.

'Yes.' A small sound of impatience coloured the word. 'Were you surprised? Happy? Upset?'

Skye tilted her head back in the water, dipping her hair completely under the surface, brushing her thick fringe back with it. 'All of the above,' she said with a shrug, lifting her head out of the water.

'And when did you decide that you wouldn't tell me?'

Skye pulled a face. 'It's not like I made a decision. I guess…' Her eyes flicked to his for a moment and then instantly jumped away. 'It didn't really occur to me that I *would* tell you.'

'No?' A simple question, but she felt the intensity of feelings that coloured it.

She pushed up straight, staring out at the ocean and wishing she were bobbing on top of it, far from her husband, her marriage, his beautiful home. Far from the desire that lashed her even as she knew she should be more sensible.

'No.'

He said nothing, but she intuited his silent judgement.

'Our marriage was over.'

'Which doesn't change the fact we made a child together.'

Skye nodded softly. 'I was upset.' She returned to the original question. 'That was my first feeling. Devastation. I couldn't believe the timing. If it had been a few weeks earlier...' She shook her head. 'I've always wanted children. Even as a teenager, I imagined myself with a big family. Lots of kids. A loving husband.' She pressed her cheek against her hands, turning to face him. 'A happy family.'

'Like you never had,' he said perceptively.

There was no sense in denying it. She'd told him enough of her upbringing for him to know that she'd been miserable. 'Yes.'

'Are you happy now?'

She shook her head slowly; the tears that sparkled on her eyes were a surprise. 'How can I be?' she whispered. 'I'm trapped. This marriage is everything I don't want. I mean, I can't wait to meet my—our—baby. I know I'm going to love him or her so much. But, Matteo, if you felt *anything* for me at all, ever...if there was anything in your motivation beyond revenge and greed...surely you can see that making me stay married to you is a mistake?'

He made a noise of frustration, closing the distance between them, his hands seeking her hips under water. He pulled her away from the edge of the pool quickly, holding her to his body, his eyes boring down into hers.

'How can you call this a mistake?'

And he kissed her then, hard, desperately, hungrily, with all the need that was thick inside him. He kissed her, and he held her close to him, and then he moved one hand away. She felt his fingers brush against her stomach as he sought the waistband of his swim shorts and pushed them downwards. His legs moved, freeing him of his impediment, and then he was naked against her, his arousal hard to her stomach.

Yearning was like wildfire, advantageous and determined. It flicked over her, demanding her attention and indulgence. It was a force too needy to ignore, and she didn't want to ignore it anyway.

But hurt was too strong to be forgotten, and he had hurt her badly.

'I hate you,' she said seriously, pulling away from him long enough to stare into his eyes, to show him that she meant it. 'This is just physical. It doesn't mean anything.'

A muscle jerked in the base of his jaw. He looked as though he wanted to say something, and for a moment she hoped he would argue; but then he nodded, pulling her to the end of the pool that was shallower so that his feet touched the bottom. And then he brought his mouth back to hers and beneath the water his fingers sought her underwear, pushing them away easily. He had barely removed them before she lifted up, wrapping her legs around his waist so that he could easily slide inside her, deep inside her.

He did so, thrusting slowly at first so that she moaned into his mouth, her fingers lifting of their own accord and tangling in his dark, wet hair.

More tears filled her eyes, thickening in her throat as memories slammed through her. The perfection of this was a cruel irony, given their emotional discordance. Yet she didn't resent it. She was grateful for it. Grateful at least for this connection.

In all her life, it was undoubtedly the most meaningful, even when it meant so very little to him.

She dropped her fingers to his shoulders, digging them into his smooth, tanned flesh, rolling her hips as he pushed deeper.

He slid his mouth down to her neck, nipping the flesh at its base, moving deeper and faster. She gripped his shoulders as the world began to fade away from her, as pleasure began to eclipse everything else, just as it always had. She tilted her head back, and her breasts surfaced above the water so that he could lean forward and catch one nipple in his mouth, flicking it with his tongue.

Her breasts were so sensitive. It tipped her over

the edge. She cried out into the night sky of Venice, the ancient sky with its prehistoric stars; she cried out, she held him and she drifted away on a wave of pleasure, on a moment of perfection. But he didn't let her come back down to earth. Even as she was trembling, he lifted her back, crushing her to his body and moving to the steps; lifting her higher; spinning her so that he could place her bottom on the edge of the pool.

He brought his mouth down to hers, pushing her backwards so that she was lying flat against the tiles that surrounded the pool. His mouth worshipped her, tasting her mouth first, then her breasts, licking the water from them at the same time he layered new needs, wants and memories across her. His tongue teased her stomach and he smiled against her belly, then dragged his mouth lower, to her womanhood, her core of femininity, lashing her once with his tongue so that she moaned and arched her back.

'Tell me what you want,' he invited, the words roughened by emotions she couldn't understand, emotions that did something new to her, something dangerous.

Skye stared upwards, her mind fuzzy, desire thick in her blood.

She wanted her husband. She wanted him kissing her, making love to her; she wanted it all.

You'll be begging me to take you...

'Tell me what *you* want,' she challenged, the words husky, her breath burning in her lungs. She pushed up on her elbows, glaring at him, her cheeks flushed, her eyes sparkling with defiance even as she was riding a wave of pleasure that was robbing her of sanity.

His smile was lightly mocking. 'Isn't it obvious?' And he brought his mouth back to her most sensitive flesh, so that she could no longer think or speak—she could only feel—and she felt *everything*. She felt the cool breeze on her flesh, the night around them; she felt the moon looking down and the stars watching on; she felt his mouth, she felt his hands, she felt her heart, she felt her raging blood.

'Please...' The word escaped her mouth before she could catch it and she bit down on her lip, hating that he had been right. That she had ended up asking him to take her once more. That she was close to begging for him.

He didn't stop.

He didn't gloat, either. And she appreciated that. She arched her back and his hands ran upwards along her sides, holding her steady, and then he pushed away, moving over her, taking her once more, thrusting inside her and answering all the questions she'd hadn't known to ask.

It was perfection, yet it was also so flawed.

As if he could read the thought, even before she

knew that she'd had it, he brought his mouth to hers. 'This has always been perfect between us.'

But it wasn't perfect!

It wasn't perfect to want someone so much when it had nothing to do with love.

All the fantasies she'd had about life and relationships and marriage and family and belonging disintegrated. Yet, maybe this was enough.

It felt like enough, being made love to by— no, having sex with—her husband. It was easy to think that everything would be wonderful for ever more.

'It's crazy,' she whispered, but she didn't stop moving beneath him, writhing, feeling, welcoming, needing.

'*Si.*' Speech was impossible as he moved faster, deeper, kissing her in time with his body's movements so that she was dancing to a rhythm all of his making.

She collapsed beneath him at the same moment he exploded and they rode that perfect wave of delight together, neither wanting to contemplate what would come next. Nor what it would mean.

CHAPTER SEVEN

'AND WHAT WE did last night is safe?' His eyes latched to hers over the spread of newspapers, coffee and croissants.

Skye's cheeks flushed at the oblique reference to the way they'd made love by the plunge pool, only metres from where they'd first slept together.

'I think it's a little late to be worrying about unwanted consequences, don't you?'

His smile was just a tight flicker of his lips. 'I mean so far as the baby is concerned.'

She laughed. 'Of course. Do you think sex might pose a threat?'

Dark colour slashed his cheeks. 'I have no clue, *cara*. It is the first time I've slept with a pregnant woman.'

She focused back on the newspaper, the headline swimming before her eyes. 'It's fine,' she said thickly. 'No risk.'

'Good.' He reached across, curving his hands over hers. 'Because I want to do more of that.'

Her pulse thumped heavily in her veins. She kept her attention averted. Didn't she want that too? Well, yes, but there was definitely a risk to *her* if she made a habit of falling into his arms.

'More swimming?' she prompted.

'Not what I meant.'

'I know.' She lifted her face, her eyes locking to his with a shyness that was at odds with what they'd shared. 'I know what you meant.'

'And I think you want it too.'

She swallowed, focusing on a point over his shoulder. 'I think we have to be careful *not* to do that again.'

His brow furrowed but she didn't see it. 'Why the hell not?'

'You want us to raise this baby together? That's hard enough without bringing sex into it.'

'We're married.' He laughed softly. 'And expecting a baby. Sex is already a part of it.'

She was quiet, uncertain what to say, and he moved the conversation along, his eyes watchful. 'Just think about it.'

She thought about pointing out that she didn't *need* to think about it. That her mind was working this morning, as it hadn't been the night before, and that sex was definitely going to complicate things unbearably.

For her, anyway.

Apparently it had never been an issue for him.

He'd been able to compartmentalise sex from the rest. From the lies. The betrayal.

'It's too complicated.'

He compressed his lips with frustration. 'I think

we established last night that *nothing* about that is complicated. It is as easy for us as ever.'

'But your heart's not at risk,' she said pointedly. 'But, for me, having loved you once makes me terrified of being stupid all over again. Of mistaking sex for something else entirely. Especially when you can make my body feel like that.' She stood up uneasily, changing the subject even when her mind was still ticking over the facts, trying to make sense of it. 'It's such a nice day. I'm going to go for a walk.'

He didn't look at her. In fact, he continued to stare straight ahead, almost as though he hadn't heard. She moved towards the door and his voice commanded her to stop.

'Wait a moment.' He stood and she held her breath, wondering if he was going to say something that might change how she felt, while knowing he couldn't. There was nothing. 'I will come with you.'

Exasperation was obvious in Skye's expression. 'That's not necessary.'

'Tell me something, Mrs Vin Santo. Is it only when I kiss you that you listen to reason?' He stood, his intent obvious as he moved towards her. He came so close, and she held her breath, waiting, knowing what was coming. Knowing she could move away, be firm.

She didn't.

She stood her ground and stared right back.

No, she did more than that. She willed him to kiss her. For his kisses didn't only take away her senses and stir her desire. They took away her pain too.

And she longed for that moment of peace. Of clarity and pleasure—of happiness.

'I don't want you trying to swim in the canals again.'

'I'll keep my land legs.'

'Perhaps.' His eyes glinted with determination. 'But I'll be there to make sure of it.'

There really never had been any sense arguing with Matteo. He always got what he wanted. Throughout their marriage, certainly, but even their marriage itself was proof of the lengths to which he'd go to achieve his aims.

She walked beside him, retracing routes that were instantly familiar to her. Paths that she'd travelled often in the past, when she'd been in love and Venice had been the physical representation of that state of mind. When she'd been keen to explore every last crevice of this beautiful city, letting its ancient stories breathe into her.

They passed a *gelateria* and she slowed a little, staring in at the beautifully arranged piles of confectionery, each colourful heap decorated with a piece of fruit or a wedge of chocolate.

'You want some?' he asked, apparently attuned to her every thought.

She bit down on her lip and nodded.

'*Bacio* still your favourite?'

The memory was one of her favourites but the cruel irony of it slapped her in the face.

Kisses.

The *gelato* she'd loved and that he'd teased her with, kissing her as he'd spelled it out, dribbling the ice-cream over her flesh as he'd kissed her everywhere.

'No,' she said quickly, shaking her head to dislodge the recollection. 'Strawberry.'

He arched a brow, perhaps understanding why she was keen to substitute a different flavour. 'If you're sure.'

He approached the vendor and she watched for a moment before turning her attention down the street. It was like so many of the little paths she loved in Venice. The water to one side, the lines of houses built so that they were all attached, though painted in different colours, all shades of yellow and orange, some pale, some bright, with window boxes overflowing with flowers. Some houses had rooftop gardens like Matteo's, and greenery bloomed overhead.

There were not many people in the street, but her eyes landed on a small boy just a little way down. He looked frightened. Her brows drew together as she looked around for an adult who might be accompanying him and saw no one.

She smiled at him encouragingly.

He didn't return it.

He could only stare.

She drew closer on autopilot, and as she got nearer she noticed new details about him. His clothes were perhaps a size too small. His jeans finished about an inch up from his ankles and his shirt just met his waistband, so that the smallest movement would drive it upwards, separating it and exposing his stomach. His hair was close-cropped.

She paused just in front of him. 'Hi.'

He blinked.

'Are you okay?' she asked in halting Italian. More memories—Matteo in bed, teaching her phrases, laughing at her mispronunciations and penalising her with kisses that made her head spin so that, in the end, she'd longed to say the words incorrectly even when she knew them by heart.

'Yes, madam,' he replied in his own tongue, then said something else. Something too fast and accented for her to understand.

Her smile was apologetic. 'I'm sorry, my Italian is not very good.'

'He said he's never seen anyone like you before.' Matteo's voice came from right behind her.

He stood, holding two *gelato* cones. He handed one to her and he passed the other to the child.

Matteo spoke in rapid-fire Italian, but she caught enough of his words to get the gist. 'Eat it. You look hungry.'

The child didn't need to be told twice. He instantly reached for the *gelato*, his grubby fingers wrapping around the cone.

'I wonder what he meant,' Skye said, looking up at Matteo.

Matteo phrased the question to the child, raising his brows at the response.

'He said you are very beautiful, and very fancy.'

Skye's cheeks flushed pink. She stood, giving Matteo her full attention. 'You're making that up.'

'Why on earth would I do that?'

'I don't know. Why do you do anything?'

The little boy's fingers reached out and ran across Skye's forearm, touching her skin gently as he murmured something in Italian. She smiled down at him, not at all concerned by the touch. Matteo, beside her, apparently didn't feel the same. He stiffened noticeably.

'He says you are very soft. Like...'

Skye held her breath. 'Like what?'

'Like a petal.'

She laughed. 'Quite the romantic, huh?' But she sobered at the look of wonderment on the little boy's face. 'Do you think he's okay? Does he need something?'

'He's Romani, most likely,' Matteo said.

'Where are his parents?'

Matteo asked the child, but compressed his lips, apparently disapproving of his wife's involvement in the child's life.

Skye didn't care. As though she could simply leave a young boy—he must have only been six or seven, if that—on the streets!

'His family have a boat near by, he says. He works from here.'

'Works?' Skye's confusion was obvious. 'He's too young to work.'

She crouched down again, dislodging the boy's grip. 'Do you need anything?' she asked in English.

He shook his head, then looked at the ice-cream, and Skye smiled.

But she wasn't convinced. She reached into her bag and pulled out several notes. She handed them to the little boy, making sure his fingers were tight around the paper. 'Take this and go home,' she said softly. 'You should be at school. *Scuola*.'

His eyes were huge. He looked at the amount in his palm and then hugged Skye, so that she laughed. 'Home,' she said gently.

He turned and ran off, his skinny little legs bowed at the knees.

Emotions lurched inside Skye. Damned pregnancy hormones.

'Are you going to rescue every impoverished child you see? If so, might I suggest we avoid St Mark's.'

She threw her husband a look of impatience. 'It's so sad. That poor little boy.'

Matteo shrugged. 'He looked happy enough to me.'

Was it any surprise to Skye that her famously cold-hearted husband hadn't been moved by the sight of the obviously hungry little boy? It was just another mark against him; another proof of his emotional detachment.

They walked in silence for a moment, Skye tasting her ice-cream, enjoying the sweetness and the relief of the cold texture on a very warm summer day. But somewhere near the Rialto Bridge she paused.

'You gave him your *gelato*.'

Matteo nodded slowly. 'So?'

'Because you thought he looked hungry too.' Skye scanned his face. 'Because you *did* care!'

Matteo's expression flashed with emotions Skye didn't recognise.

'And they say you don't have a heart.'

'I have a heart, *cara*,' he promised. And her own stuttered to a stop, thumping hard in her chest. 'And our baby will know that.' He dropped his mouth towards hers and for a second she held her breath, expecting another kiss. *Needing* the gesture that was so simple and so complicated all at once.

But instead he took a bite off the top of her ice-cream, and she laughed instinctively, automatically. 'Hey! I'm eating for two, don't you know?'

He straightened, a smile in his eyes so obvious that her stomach flipped and flopped with warmth and with…*love*. She squashed the feeling.

She didn't want it.

That knowledge sobered her.

'I wonder what our child will be like,' she said distractedly as they moved closer to the Grand Canal.

'Can you imagine him or her?'

'I sometimes have a dream,' she said with a shrug of her slender shoulders. 'I can see a little baby. Chubby with caramel skin like yours—dark eyes, dimples.' She shrugged again. 'But I guess all babies are a bit like that.'

'It is how I picture our child too. A little girl with a fringe like yours.'

'I don't think babies are born with hair styles,' she pointed out. 'You think it will be a girl?'

He pulled a face. 'I don't know. I don't care.'

'Really? And here I had you pegged for one of those patriarchal guys who would be all about the male heir.'

He dug his hands into his pocket. 'I was not close to my father,' he said after a long silence, one that was heavy with his own reflections and memories. 'My grandfather more or less raised me. Perhaps if I had seen a different example of father and son bonding I might yearn more for a son of my own.' His lips twisted into a dismissive smile. 'As it is, I just want our child to be healthy. And to have his mother's heart.'

'Yeah? Why is that?'

'According to you, I don't have one,' he pointed out.

'That's according to everyone,' she corrected, and began walking once more. One foot in front of the other. Trying not to think about his heart and their baby growing inside her. Nor to think about the way *he'd* moved inside her only the night before.

'*Si.* And what do you think, Skye? Am I as heartless as everyone says?'

Her face paled. 'I don't think you should ask me that.'

'Because your answer would hurt my feelings?'

'Perhaps,' she whispered. 'Does it matter what I think?'

He was quiet for a moment, his expression serious, and then he smiled as though physically pushing the conversation aside. 'I'm hungry. Shall we lunch?'

'Didn't we just finish breakfast?'

He made a *tsk*ing noise of disapproval. 'And you say you are eating for two! Breakfast was hours ago.' He reached down and wrapped his fingers around her hand, lifting the ice-cream cone to his lips while his eyes held hers. He took another bite.

Skye's heart throbbed at the simple gesture of intimacy.

Really, in the scheme of things it meant nothing, yet it made her soul soar. Happiness was right in front of her and his smile was telling her to grab it.

But his smile lied.

It always had done.

Maybe he couldn't help it.

She wasn't going to risk being hurt again just to find out.

'Lunch sounds good,' she said, as if pulling a rain cloud over the sunshine of their banter of only seconds ago. The words were cold and damp. Sensible.

Safe.

'Which way?' she asked, swapping her *gelato* to the other hand to prevent any further incursions. Any new suggestions of an intimacy that was fraudulent.

He looked at her for a moment, long and hard, then turned back to the path in front of them. 'Not much further. This way.'

They walked in silence, but it was no longer comfortable. It was thick with the doubts and frustrations that were, undoubtedly, to become the hallmarks of their relationship.

After almost ten minutes, Matteo slowed. 'Here.'

Skye paused, looking in the direction he'd cocked his head, and she expelled a breath of uncertainty. 'Here?'

'Something wrong with it?'

She took in the crisp white table cloths, the small vases with carnations in each one, the enormous chandeliers that looked to line the dining room, the pianist in the corner playing what she thought to be Bach.

'It's just a little more formal than I'd expected.'

'I'm sure they will fix you a sandwich, if you would prefer.'

It was another breath from the past. The memory of how he'd teased her mercilessly about her love for cucumber sandwiches, something he found bland and so quintessentially British.

'Fine,' she said with a furrowed brow, moving ahead of him into the beautiful restaurant.

A man in a tuxedo greeted them, his brows thick and dark, his hair grey. After a short conversation with Matteo in fluent Italian, the waiter directed them into the restaurant. It was so much grander, and more beautiful, from inside.

From this vantage point, Skye could see that the tables were propped beneath windows that looked out over the Grand Canal, and the stately Rialto Bridge as it spanned one side to the other. There were window boxes at each window filled with pretty pink azaleas, and the floor was tiled with shimmering black and white marble. Several waiters and waitresses stood waiting to serve, all in elegant crisp white shirts and black tuxedo jackets, and, like a butler parody brought to life, one stood with a silver tray balanced on top of his white-gloved palm.

'This way, madam,' the waiter said, and Skye realised she'd been frozen in time.

What was wrong with her? It wasn't as though she'd never been in such a beautiful restaurant. She'd grown up with the proverbial silver spoon. She'd had more birthdays in places like this than she could remember.

But being here with Matteo, the strains of world-class piano music reaching them, the flowers moving gently in the breeze, was all so… *romantic*.

The word whispered itself through her soul and she did her best to push it aside. She kept a neutral expression on her features as she strode through the restaurant, taking the seat opposite Matteo and wishing she'd worn something a little fancier than jeans and a grey T-shirt. At least her jewellery gave the ensemble an air of formality; the clunky gold and green necklace was one of a kind and matched her manicure. A manicure she'd had done when she'd imagined that she'd be flying off to Australia single, pregnant and far away from Matteo and his manipulations. She eyed her nails with a small frown.

'Yes,' he said slowly, as she sat down. 'I've been thinking the same thing.'

Her heartbeat accelerated wildly. 'What's that?'

He reached into the pocket of his jacket and lifted out a small box. She recognised it instantly. Her back was straight but her spine tingled with apprehension and misgivings.

He flicked it open and slid the box across to her, with considerably less fanfare than the last time he'd presented a ring box for her inspection.

'Nothing would make me happier than if you'd agree to marry me, Skye. Say you will.'

The words seemed to glisten in the air around her, dancing and lifting her up. She nodded with all the enthusiasm that her heart gave rise to. 'Of course I will!'

'I don't like seeing you without it on,' he said with a shrug.

Skye reached for the box but made no effort to liberate the ring inside. She ran her finger over the huge diamond, remembering how her first re-action had been one of mixed feelings. Delight, euphoria and bliss at the thought of marrying Matteo Vin Santo, whom she had loved from almost the moment they'd met. But disappointment too that he'd thought her pretentious enough to want a ring such as this. She supposed it was the fact she was a billion-pound heiress, that people presumed she was used to expensive items and only valued those things that had a high material cost.

It wasn't true, though. Skye had always shied away from ostentation and visible signs of wealth.

'You don't like it, do you?' he asked quietly, his eyes reading every nuanced expression that crossed her face.

She lifted startled eyes to his. 'I… It's… It feels a little like a prison sentence now,' she said with a shake of her head. 'That's all.'

'Now who's the liar?' he countered silkily, suspending the conversation when another waiter appeared.

'Good afternoon, madam, sir. I… Oh! *Scusa—mi dispiace!* I'm so sorry! I'm interrupting a special moment. My apologies…'

'It's fine,' Skye hastened to reassure him.

'I go, I go. I give you time.'

Skye watched the man leave, perplexed, and then turned her attention to Matteo. He hadn't moved. His attention was still on Skye's face, watchful and attentive. 'Why didn't you tell me?'

She knew what he meant and didn't bother to obfuscate. 'You chose it,' she said with a shrug. And now she lifted the ring out, holding it between her forefinger and thumb. 'I used to love it for that reason alone.'

'But it's not what you would have chosen?'

'I would never have wanted to choose my own ring.' She fixed him with a determined gaze. 'In hindsight, it should have told me how little you knew me.'

His lips twisted with mockery. Directed at her, or himself?

He reached across, retrieving the ring from her hands and sliding it back onto her ring finger. 'Wear it until I arrange a replacement.'

Her blood bubbled and swirled. A replacement spoke of such permanence. And in the meantime?

She stared down at the enormous diamond—a diamond that had kept her company all the time she'd been married to Matteo, a diamond she had thought she would wear for ever, and felt a hint of disloyalty. 'Perhaps we can have it turned into a pendant. If it's a daughter, she can have it for her sixteenth birthday.'

His eyes held a sparkle she didn't understand. 'Certainly. Or we can sell it for our son's first car.'

'God, this is really happening, isn't it?'

'Yes, *cara*. It is.'

'You seem so glad about that.'

He shrugged. 'Having not planned it does not make the news less welcome.'

'You didn't want children.'

'You are so sure of that?'

She nodded. 'You said so.'

A frown pulled at his features. 'You are twenty-two years old, Skye. I cannot think what I was doing at twenty-two, but it was not raising a child.'

'You were running your business,' she pointed out. 'In fact, you had been doing so for several years.'

'You remember so clearly.'

Her cheeks flooded with peach. Of course she remembered. She remembered everything he'd ever said, as though he'd imprinted his words against the iron of her soul, branding her for all time.

'So it's not like you were out being all irresponsible or anything. You were working hard.'

'I was doing both,' he said seriously. 'I worked hard. Played harder.'

Jealousy fired through her and she hated it. For one thing, she'd still been a child when he had been twenty-two. There was no way she could be threatened by the fact he'd had relationships before her.

The waiter appeared silently, and another waitress behind him who carried a tray with champagne flutes; champagne and a platter of food.

'Compliments of the establishment,' the waiter murmured, placing the food and drinks down, bowing low and then disappearing.

'I suppose it would be rude to tell him we don't want champagne?'

He ignored her question. 'I didn't think having children made sense.' He shrugged. 'But that decision is now out of my hands.'

She tilted her face away, staring out at the Grand Canal and the hustle and bustle of Venice in the afternoon.

It was a city like no other.

Its character changed so completely depending on what time of day it was. Now, in the early afternoon, the *strada* were crowded with tourists, big and happy, wearing hats and cameras and beaming smiles, talking loudly and laughing and eating as they walked, making their way back to the cruise terminal, ready to continue their tour of Europe.

Come night time, the streets would be filled with Venetians, promenading elegantly, speaking quietly, their voices taking on a musical quality as they lulled against the canals.

'Of course it's not…ideal,' she said jerkily. 'I meant what I said when I came to see you. I want a divorce.' Her voice wobbled and she forced herself to be calm, digging her nails into her palms. 'But I can understand why you want to give this a chance.' She swallowed. 'So I think we should try this. Try to make it work. For the baby's sake.'

His eyes held a quality that filled her with something strange. Emotions were rioting beneath her skin. 'A real marriage?'

'No.' Her smile was wistful. 'It will never be that. We'll both know that it's just for our son or daughter. But I'll stop fighting this. I'll try to make a life here. A life outside of you.' She breathed out softly then turned to face him. 'But if I'm miserable, I'll go. And I will trust that deep down, beneath the way you are, beyond being ruthless and determined and cold, there is a good man who will be reasonable and treat me with respect, for the sake of our child.' She tilted her chin at a defiant angle, and Matteo was silent. The champagne bottle sat between them, mocking the seriousness of their discussion with its frothy enthusiasm.

'So pragmatic,' he murmured after a long pause. Was Skye imagining the way his words were deepened by emotion?

'I took a page out of your book,' she volleyed back.

'You perfected it, it would appear.'

Matteo stared out at the canal, his expression sombre.

How could he argue with such impeccable

logic? He couldn't. For all his bluster and bravado, had he really expected he'd keep Skye locked up in his house forever? Had he thought he could threaten her with a custody battle and that she'd give up her life and freedom to be in a marriage that made her miserable?

It wasn't as though he could outgun her on the legal side. She had endless resources and a great reputation. If anything, attacking her in the courts would backfire badly, given her age and philanthropic history. And his reputation as a cold, heartless bastard.

'Matteo? You're a thousand miles away.'

He blinked, drawing his attention back to Skye. She was lifting a final spoonful of the dessert to her lips. Lips that were pink and full and that drew his gaze as a flower did a bee.

His stomach lurched. Desire, unfathomable, irrepressible desire, swarmed him.

'I was thinking about the bridge,' he said after a moment's pause.

'The Rialto?'

He nodded, a gruff shift of his head. 'You know, it took a heap of money to build. They had to get funds from lots of different sources. There was even a sort of early iteration of the lottery that raised money for its construction.'

Skye tilted her head to the side. 'I didn't know that.'

'I was thinking that sometimes taking a gamble on something pays off. Sometimes it can lead to something unique and lasting.' He turned his attention back to her. 'Don't you think?'

CHAPTER EIGHT

SKYE SHIFTED UNCOMFORTABLY in her seat, keeping her discomfort hidden from her husband's all-seeing gaze.

Only, Matteo did see the way she winced, and leaned forward. 'What is it?'

'Nothing,' Skye said, a tight smile on her face. 'I just walked too far today, that's all.' This day, and every day for the last week, since they'd taken to strolling around Venice each morning, afterwards stopping somewhere new for lunch.

Conversation was limited to unsensational topics, like the weather or current events or politics; nothing that they disagreed on. Nothing that could remind Skye that they were enemies, really, beneath the romance of Venice and the fact they were going to become parents.

But deep down she knew they were pretending again. At least they both knew the rules this time.

And Matteo seemed determined to stick to them. After the night on the terrace, he hadn't said or done anything out of line. Not a word of seduction, not a hint of flirtation. He'd been the perfect gentleman.

'You're in pain?'

'No, no.' She winced again. 'Just a little. It's my lower back, that's all. It's an occupational hazard of the whole pregnancy thing.'

'We've been pushing it.' His words were tinged with self-recrimination. 'I'm sorry.'

'It's hardly your fault,' Skye said, her brows drawn together. 'I'm the one who keeps suggesting we go out.'

He held his expression neutral but there was a hint of something she didn't understand that danced in the edges of his eyes. 'I was foolish to let you walk so much.'

'*Let* me?' Skye countered. 'Remember that whole "me being an autonomous human being" thing? Remember how I have that small thing called free will?'

Again, his eyes flicked with something she didn't understand and then he stood, moving around the dinner table, extending his hands to her.

'What is it?' She looked at him, lifting her hands into his, the brightness of her diamond glinting in the pale light of the room.

'Let me help you.'

'I'm fine,' she demurred, instantly pushing against whatever help he had in mind.

'What's the matter, Skye? Are you afraid of what might happen if I touch you?'

She swallowed past the lump in her throat, her eyes holding his. She was terrified.

Terrified of how badly she wanted him. The week they'd spent trawling all over Venice, exploring it anew, had been like the honeymoon they'd never had. It was the other piece of the puzzle. After their wedding, they'd had sex. A lot of sex. And she'd thought that was intimacy. But walking side by side, not touching, just talking, had been different.

It had been a form of torturous foreplay and, yes, she was afraid of what would happen if he touched her. But she stood anyway, not blinking, not doing anything to convey that fear.

'Lie down.' He nodded towards one of the long couches that sat opposite them. She nodded, moving across the room with the grace that was innate to her.

'You don't have to do this...'

'You're uncomfortable because of *my* baby. Of course I have to help you. It is my duty.'

Again, his insistence on his *duty* filled her with a cold ache—it served as a reminder of the fact he viewed her as an obligation. A responsibility. She kept her face averted as she lay down on her stomach, tilting her head to look out towards the view. She could see only the flower pots, an explosion of geraniums in the pale moonlight.

His hands on her back were gentle.

He knelt at her side and ran his fingers over her with just enough pressure to bring a sense of immediate relief.

'May I lift your shirt?' The words were throaty and deep.

Skye's eyes were drawn to his. 'Yes.'

He pushed the fabric up slowly and she held her breath. It was just a few inches, enough for him to be able to massage her naked flesh. But it was skin-to-skin contact and it rocked her world. She bit down on her lower lip and shut her eyes, surrendering to the sensations that were rioting through her.

'What's this from?' He drew his finger over her skin, tracing a very pale imperfection that ran in a semi-circular shape.

'A dog bite,' Skye murmured, sleepy and relaxed. 'When I was twelve.'

She didn't see him frown. 'It only bit you here?'

Skye stifled a yawn. 'Yes. He was old and quite crazy, really. He'd got a fright and I was sitting on the floor, right beside him. He gave me a fright, let me tell you.'

'I didn't know you had a dog.'

'He wasn't mine,' Skye murmured, shifting a little. Her back was feeling much better but she didn't tell Matteo that. He continued to move his palms over her flesh and she didn't want him to stop. Ever. 'He was my great-aunt's.'

Matteo's hands were still for a moment. 'She raised you after your father died?'

'Yeah.' Another yawn. 'She had seven dogs. Apparently she had a penchant for taking in strays. I was her last, though.'

'You were hardly a stray,' Matteo pointed out. 'Are you close to her?'

'She passed away three years ago,' Skye said crisply, closing the conversation out of habit.

'Were you close to her? Before she died,' Matteo pushed, either not comprehending her cues or not caring about them.

Skye tossed the words around in her mind, making sense of them, listening to them as if she were an outsider. 'She raised me,' Skye said after a long pause. 'I'm very grateful to her.'

But Matteo wasn't fooled by Skye's selective choice of language. She was hiding something, and that rankled. More than it should, given their relationship, or lack thereof. What had he expected? That she'd suddenly open up and confide all her deep and dark secrets to him?

She certainly wouldn't now. But how come they'd never discussed this before, when they'd first married? Why hadn't he asked more questions?

Because he hadn't wanted to know.

Skye had simply been a means to an end, not

a person with her own thoughts, feelings, history and sadness.

The realisation wasn't new, yet it sat strangely in his chest, like an accusation lined with barbed wire. He'd looked at her and seen the hotel.

He gazed down on his wife and a tight smile cracked his lips as he saw that she had fallen asleep. With her dark hair and pink cheeks and pale skin, her red lips shaped like two perfect rose petals. She was his own Snow White.

Only he was no Prince Charming. Prince Charming would never have married her for a hotel. To avenge a theft that had taken place years earlier. And he certainly wouldn't have black-mailed her into staying married.

His smile faded as he reached for her gently, lifting her as though she weighed nothing, and cradling her to his chest.

She stirred a little, lifting a hand to him, but then she relaxed, a smile on her face.

He lifted his gaze, staring straight ahead as he carried her through the house and up the stairs, to the solitude of her own room.

Skye's dreams were of Matteo. Of the night they'd met—the night she'd fallen in love. Her dreams were of their conversations, the words he'd offered her that had been more special than gold dust. 'I don't believe in fairy tales,' she'd told him the day after they'd met, when the mirage of a fairy tale had hovered on her horizon. She hadn't dared try to grab it. Reaching for perfection resulted in pain.

'Even when you're living one?' he'd pushed, pressing his lips to her cheek so that her stomach had lurched, her heart had thumped and her body had gone into sensory meltdown.

'There's no such thing.' She'd learned that lesson years ago. Her mother had deserted her. Her father had never bothered to get to know her. Her great-aunt had avoided affection as though it were a sign of personal weakness to care for another human. Boarding school had been more a prison than a Hogwarts. 'There's just real life.'

'But sometimes real life can be every bit as perfect as a fairy tale, no?'

Her dreams were of their first kiss, his proposal, their wedding, their first time together. All the times thereafter. The fairy tale she'd thought she was living. A fairy tale that had been a nightmare, in all ways but one. He'd betrayed her and he'd broken her heart, but his body called to hers. Nothing would change that.

She moaned in her bed, arching her back, and she could feel the ghost of his hands on her. A phantom touch that was a torment because it was not real. She stretched her hands out, instinctively seeking him, and not finding him. She reached for him and didn't connect with flesh.

The sense of loss was instant and it was sharp. She stood on autopilot, still groggy from sleep, her body in complete charge. She moved through his home with no idea of the time. It could have been midnight, or it could have been the early hours of the morning. It didn't matter.

She contemplated knocking on his door, but didn't. She pushed it inwards, hovering on the threshold.

There was no such thing as fairy tales. She'd been right. That wasn't what this was. But he was her husband and in that moment she needed him with a ferocity that wouldn't be quelled. He was asleep in bed. She tiptoed across the floorboards and then rolled her eyes.

Was she afraid of waking him? Wasn't that kind of the point?

Still, she crept towards the bed, pausing for a moment to study him.

He was a stunning specimen of masculinity but, asleep like this, she felt all his vulnerabilities as well. She could see the man he was and the boy he'd been. She could see all the parts of him and her heart lurched with recognition of the fact that she loved all those parts. His arrogance. His determination. Even his ruthlessness. For these aspects all made Matteo who he was.

She moved quietly but quickly, shedding her clothes, thinking she should have done it before she made her way to his room, then she pushed the sheet back and straddled him, dropping her mouth to his and kissing him.

He made a low moan from deep in his throat and his hands lifted, catching her face and holding her still so that his eyes could latch to hers. His room was dark but there was enough light cast by the moon and the lights beyond the villa for them to see one another. He stared at her for a moment, at her face, her lips that were parted in expectation, her eyes that were hooded with desire and her body that was naked, needing him.

'I want you,' she said simply and he groaned once more, dropping his hands to her hips and positioning her so that she could slide onto his length and take him deep inside.

She tilted her head to the ceiling at the feeling, so welcome, so familiar, so perfect. Her body was on fire. Every nerve ending was dancing inside her, quivering with the rightness of his touch. She dropped forward, bringing her mouth to his, kissing him hungrily as he moved inside her. She rolled her hips, her rhythm desperate and fast, her needs insatiable, and he laughed softly, nodding against her head.

'I know.'

He caught her at the waist and rolled her easily, breaking their bodies apart. And, though it was a brief separation, it was enough for Skye to issue a sound of complaint that had him laughing once more, softly, a short sound that filled her with impatience. But then he was back, moving into her deeper, harder, his body taking control of hers and commanding their desire; building it up, wrapping it around them, making her tremble and writhe beneath him as pleasure built and built inside her, stretching like a coil that wouldn't be contained.

She cried out as it reached fever pitch and then broke across her. She dug her nails into his shoulders and held on for dear life, hoping it would save her. The galaxy was around her, cosmic and beautiful, and she was flying through it, just a piece of flotsam, a heavenly, bliss, pleasure-filled piece of flotsam.

He dropped his mouth to her breasts and took one into his mouth, rolling his tongue over her nipple as his fingers sought the other, tormenting it between his forefinger and thumb. Her breasts ached for him and he knew that. He pushed deeper inside her and she sobbed—it was a sob of relief. Of joy. Of gratitude.

It was also a sob of fear.

What hope did she have of controlling her emotions when there was this to contend with? It didn't matter if she called it 'having sex' or 'sleeping together' or 'making love'. A rose by any other name...

She was making love. Every touch, every movement, every sensation, was binding her with the emotion and she would never be free of that.

'I loved you so much,' she said, the words not exactly what she wanted to say, yet they were a reflection of what she was thinking, feeling, needing him to know.

Another explosion built, starting deep in her abdomen and spreading to the far reaches of her body, carrying delirium in its wake so that her fingertips tingled and she burst apart with pleasure. He kissed her harder and then he joined her, the rapture holding them both, wrapping around them with the same sense of urgency and euphoric release. Their breathing was in unison. Hard and fast, it filled the room. He pulled away a little, his eyes heavy as they surveyed her.

'That was a nice surprise,' he murmured minutes later, once their breath had slowed and a hint of normality had returned to the room.

She didn't say anything. She was a tangle of feelings that had gone from delight to despair in the space of seconds. The same desire that was beautiful and mesmerising was also a trap. It was a torment.

She looked at him and then turned her face.

'Are you okay?' The question was filled with such tenderness that her heart splintered off, new shards joining the old.

'I am now,' she bluffed, bravado brightening her

voice. He rolled off her but pulled her to him, holding her back to his chest, his arm curled around her body in a gesture of intimacy that hadn't even belonged in their marriage. She lay against him, her body curled like a conch shell, her eyes on the moonlit wallpaper opposite, her heart breaking as she felt his beating, hard and resolute.

Determined.

The problem with whatever the hell they'd just done was that everything felt so perfect. In contrast to the reality of their situation, when she was in his arms, when his body was buried in hers, she could believe that they *were* in a fairy tale.

The ending, the inevitable realisation that it *wasn't* perfect, was like being dropped into the middle of a war zone. Remembering that only a week and a half earlier she'd stormed her way into his office demanding a divorce—a divorce he had agreed to!—was like being doused in cold water.

Slowly, once sleep had claimed him firmly in its grasp, she wriggled away from his warmth, moving to the opposite side of the bed at first and flipping on her side to look at him as he slept.

His breathing was even, his expression relaxed. He wasn't tormented by the emotional barrenness of their marriage.

He didn't care about it.

He didn't want anything from her.

Except for the hotel.

And now the baby.

And, yes, sex.

That was what their marriage boiled down to for him.

She had to find a way to remember that. Then, she'd be okay. Wouldn't she?

'I had an incredible dream last night.' The words were drawled and deep, murmured from across the table where they were eating breakfast.

'I think I had the same dream,' she responded without looking at him. It was easier to play it light, to be cool and relaxed when she wasn't looking at him.

She turned her attention back to the paper, skimming the news without really taking any of it in. Silence returned and she was momentarily mollified by it. She sipped her coffee, replacing it carefully on the table. His hand reached out and covered hers, and her pulse kicked up a notch.

'Why did you leave?'

Skye's gaze jolted to his. 'When?'

'Last night.'

She looked down at the paper again. 'Was I meant to stay?'

'It was late. You must have been tired.'

She looked at him briefly, holding his gaze with what she hoped passed as unconcern, then gave the paper her attention once more. As if to underscore that she was in fact reading, and not just staring at a collection of words on the page, she pulled her hand free from his and turned a page. 'I sleep better in my own bed.'

'You never had a problem in my room before…'

Skye swallowed. He wasn't going to let this rest, apparently. She forced herself to meet his eyes and dropped the act. Her face was stern, her voice not a tone that invited argument. 'I don't want that.'

His eyes roamed her face thoughtfully. 'You won't sleep in my bed, but you'll come to my room when you want sex in the middle of the night?'

She nodded slowly. 'Yeah.'

'So I am like…a booty call?' he prompted, wiggling his brows so that she laughed—a laugh borne of relief that he had dropped his inquisition.

'Yep.'

He shook his head. 'Mmm, but then when I wake up wanting you, you are not within reach.'

'And you can't walk down the corridor, as I did?'

'Ah.' His eyes drew together. 'Your advances are always welcome. I cannot be certain that you would feel the same if I were to reciprocate with a midnight intrusion.'

Skye's cheeks flamed. 'I thought you wanted to make me beg for you,' she reminded him, and had the satisfaction of seeing something darken his eyes.

'I haven't done too well at that, have I?'

Skye arched a brow. 'Looking for compliments?'

'No.' He was serious. 'I'm glad you came to me last night, Skye.'

Her throat thickened and she looked away, her eyes suspiciously moist. Stupid pregnancy hormones making her emotions haywire! 'It was the massage,' she said with a shrug.

'Then you shall have massages often.' She turned back to him just in time to see him wink. Her chest compressed as though cement were being pressed against it. 'But today? You are my prisoner in other ways.'

She paused, her expression showing curiosity.

'Today, you rest. You relax and tell me what you need. I will bring you anything your heart desires.'

She nodded, but deep down she knew he could never do that. What her heart desired, really desired, wasn't on offer from Matteo Vin Santo, and never would be.

CHAPTER NINE

SKYE PUSHED THE dress onto the hanger, adding it to the collection she was gathering in one side of the dressing room. She paused, midway through reaching for the next option, staring at her reflection in the mirror. Her stomach, usually so flat, was thicker around the middle. Not round yet.

Just…different.

Her breasts had changed too. They were no longer neat and modest, and her bras had begun to pinch her sides painfully. It was enough to make her feel uncomfortable in her usual wardrobe. She ran her hands down her body, curling her fingertips over her flesh, breathing in deeply as though she could hear the little life inside her, if only she listened hard enough.

This was really happening.

Her smile was bright. She saw the joy in her face and it made her heart lurch.

Be careful, Skye. Don't forget that this isn't perfect. *It's not a fairy tale.*

But the baby was pretty damned close. All her life, she'd never known true love. She thought she'd found it with Matteo, but she'd been wrong there.

The baby would love her, though, and she would love him. With her whole heart. She would never, ever let him be hurt or sad, or feel alone or frightened. She lifted the final dress over her head, pulling it down, studying it from all angles before nodding and removing it.

She pulled her own shirt back on then tossed the new clothes over her arm and shouldered out of the changing room.

Matteo stood out like a sore thumb, waiting in the middle of the boutique, dressed in a dark suit. But he was holding something in his hands. As she got closer, her heart skidded against her rib cage. It was a soft toy.

A toy for their child.

'I thought he would need something,' Matteo said with a shrug and a bemused smile.

Skye smiled back but turned away quickly, feeling the now-familiar prick of tears threatening. She laid the dresses onto the counter in time to see the shop assistant practically wipe her drool from the side of her mouth, staring at Matteo as though he were *gelato* on a hot summer's day.

Skye understood.

She'd felt like that plenty of times.

'All this?' the assistant asked in heavily accented English.

'And the toy,' Skye said with a nod. She waited while the assistant rung the clothes up and bagged them, and then Matteo slid his credit card across, something which both surprised and frustrated Skye.

'You're buying my clothes now?' she enquired silkily as they stepped out of the boutique.

'You only need new clothes because of my baby.' His response was filled with infuriating logic.

'My baby too.'

'Yes, *cara.* I am aware of that. But it helps me feel…involved,' he said with a shrug of his shoulders and a degree of honesty that made her gut clench.

'Do you *not* feel involved otherwise?'

'No, I mean, you get to grow the baby and all the work is yours for now. Delivery, nursing.' He shrugged. 'I want to do something too.'

She would never have thought he would feel that way. She chanced a sidelong glance at his profile and then looked straight ahead as they walked down the busy street. Tourists flocked around them.

'You know, we haven't talked about a nursery,' she said thoughtfully. 'That's something you could help with.'

His whole face lit up. 'Why had I not thought of this?'

Skye burst out laughing. 'Uh-oh. Why do I feel like I've just made a very dangerous suggestion?'

'You think three bedrooms will be enough?'

She shook her head. 'One bedroom is definitely fine. And near mine.'

'Ours,' he said softly. He reached down and captured her hand. 'I would like you to be in my room again, Skye.'

Danger lurked in the softly spoken statement. She made a small gesture of demur, knowing she could never concede that intimacy again. 'Then we'll both be waking up at all hours. Separate rooms are better.' She tried to make the statement as light as possible, so that he wouldn't know how her heart had thundered at the idea of surrendering all of herself to this marriage once again.

'We'll need a room for the nanny,' he murmured, apparently still running a million miles an hour, planning for their baby in a whole new way now. One that Skye found, frankly, a tiny bit scary.

'Hold up.' She lifted a hand, pausing, turning to face him. 'What nanny?'

'You think we'll need two? Perhaps a day nanny and a night nanny. How does this work?'

'No, no, no. No nanny.'

Matteo's expression showed confusion. 'Skye, you don't have to do this without help.'

'You think I *can't* do it?'

His sigh was exasperated. 'That's not what I meant.'

'Because I'm going to be a great mother.' She froze. 'Aren't I?' Suddenly she was dizzy, hot and cold. She moved away from him, towards the wall of a building. She propped herself against it; panic pursued her. 'Oh, God. What if I'm not?' Her eyes were huge when they met his.

'You are going to be an excellent mother,' he said, moving closer, his large body framing hers.

'But you don't know that. I don't know that. I didn't... I never even knew my mother. I had a succession of stepmothers and wasn't close to any of them. I have no idea what being a mother actually means. What if I'm terrible? What if I shout? What if I'm impatient? What if I don't know the rules? Oh, God, Matteo. I'm not going to be any good at this.'

His face showed his confusion, and also a hint of amusement that she deeply resented.

'This isn't funny.' She groaned. 'I got so caught up in how much I'd love this baby that I never really thought about whether or not I'd be able to give our baby what it needs. What if I can't?'

'Skye?'

'I have no clue what time babies should go to sleep. Or kids. What about when he's older and he wants to watch a scary movie?'

'Skye?'

'And food? What do babies eat? What if I poison our child? What if I *choke* our child?'

'How are you going to choke it?' He stifled a laugh.

'I don't know! By feeding it caramel when it's two months old. I don't know!'

He dropped his mouth to hers, suffocating the words that were tumbling out of her on a wave of panic. It was a kiss of reassurance, a kiss of kindness. He kissed her and she responded, her body leaning towards his, her fingers splaying wide across his shirt. His legs, so strong and firm, stood on either side of her body, effectively imprisoning her against the wall.

'We're going to need a nanny,' she said into his mouth, the certainty that she didn't want to do this alone absolute in her mind.

'No.' He shook his head. 'I was wrong. We can get one later, if you feel it is necessary. If you want more freedom. Or if the baby isn't sleeping and you need a rest. But I will be here. I will be holding your hand, just as you will be holding mine. This isn't just your child, your responsibility. It's mine too. We're in it together.'

Slightly reassured, but still not convinced, she nodded. 'Maybe we should just meet with a few agencies. Just in case.'

'If you'd like,' he shrugged. 'Skye?'

She blinked up at him.

'You are going to be a terrific mother. You are already so in love with our baby. That's the most important thing by far.' His eyes scanned her face. 'I am sorry that you never felt that from your own mother.'

His words were precious. They meant the world to Skye. She didn't know if he was right or not, but having his support was so important.

'What if I'm not?'

'You will be.' His confidence did something strange inside of Skye. It tied knots around her heart, knots that made everything seem fine, good and safe. But there was danger in that safety, because it was so like the happiness she'd felt before. The happiness that had filled her heart and made her believe that their marriage was everything she'd been waiting for.

That he was the answer to questions she didn't even know she had.

Her smile was guarded. She nodded slowly, mentally putting essential distance between them. Their past lay before her—quicksand that could devour her at any point if she didn't take care.

'Matteo?'

'*Si?*'

She turned away from the wall, walking once more. Slowly. Thoughtfully. 'Tell me about our families.'

She didn't look up at him, so didn't see the way his expression tightened. The way his lips dragged downwards with sour memories. 'What would you like to know?'

Skye turned her fingers into the handle of the carrier bag. 'I don't know. I guess everything. My dad's lawyer didn't have all the details.'

'What did he say?'

'Only that your mother had been engaged to my father. That she met your dad and it was… love at first sight. That she ran away with him in the middle of the night.' Skye shrugged.

'*Si.*' Matteo nodded warily. 'Your father was young and arrogant. He couldn't accept that your mother preferred my father. So he made her life miserable.'

'Miserable how?' Skye prompted, thinking of her father, and frowning when she could hardly call his face to mind.

'He moved to Italy and turned up everywhere my parents went. When my mother conceived me, and your father began to accept that it was over, he turned to the business. It was a tough time for my grandfather—he had expanded too quickly and the global markets faltered. He was vulnerable and your father acted on that.'

'How?' Skye pushed.

'He actively acquired my grandfather's competitors and then drove my grandfather's businesses into the ground. Nonno borrowed heavily to prop up his failing business interests but it was not enough. Eventually, he had to sell almost everything.'

'Including the hotel,' Skye murmured.

'Your father didn't want my grandfather's businesses.' His tone was grave. 'He wanted simply to destroy them. To take something good and strong and ruin it just because he could.'

Skye's eyes glistened with shame at the description of her father's actions. Actions that made her wish Matteo was wrong. But she knew he wasn't. Strange that she could trust him so implicitly on this matter when he'd proven himself to be just as duplicitous.

Matteo stared at her long and hard for a moment before allowing the conversation to move onwards. 'The bankruptcy broke him. I went to live with him around the time it was happening. I saw a man who was proud and intelligent, who had worked hard all his life, be destroyed by the actions of your father.'

The hatred in the words chilled Skye to the core. But what could she say to refute it?

'My father used to talk about a woman he had loved. I suppose it was your mother. I think losing her destroyed him, in the same way your grandfather's business losses—'

'No.' Matteo's interruption was swift, his rebuke absolute. 'You cannot compare the two. My parents fell in love. There was nothing malicious in what they did. Your father spent a decade tearing my family's wealth apart. It was his sole mission. He was motivated solely by revenge and hatred.'

'Isn't that a little like the pot calling the kettle black?' Skye murmured. The pleasant atmosphere of only moments ago had turned dark and uncomfortable. She felt the animosity of their past, the tension that had dogged her in the first days of their second attempt at marriage, and it was back with a vengeance.

She stopped walking and looked in both directions of the street. 'I'm a little tired,' she said, not completely without truth.

Matteo studied her, as though he could see the truth of what she was saying if he looked hard enough. 'Skye?' He lifted a hand as though to touch her cheek but held it wide of her face, his expression confused. 'What happened between them has no bearing on us.'

'How can you say that?' The words were heavy with feelings. 'Everything we are is because of them. Everything.'

She wouldn't cry.

She wouldn't.

But her hand lifted to her stomach, pressing against it gently. 'This baby deserves better than to be born into so much hate.'

'There is no hate here.'

'Yes, there is.' Her eyes laced to his, and she

forced herself to see all angles. To remember everything they were—everything they'd been. 'My father hated your father. Your grandfather hated my father. You hated my father. Everyone hated everyone.'

'I don't hate you,' he said simply.

She looked away from him.

'And you don't hate me.'

That was true. She didn't hate him. She didn't know what she felt for him.

'I hate what you did.' The words were gravelled. 'I hate what you did to me. I hate what you're capable of. I hate what you took away from me. I hate that… I hate that…'

She swept her eyes shut, unable to finish the sentence.

'Go on,' he prompted.

But it was too awful. Even to *think*, let alone to say!

'I hate…'

'Yes?'

'I wish I was having this baby with anyone but you,' she finished finally, thinking it was marginally better than to admit the truth of her thoughts—that she hated that she was having a baby with Matteo. That they were to be bound together for the rest of their days.

He was silent, staring at her for so long that she wondered if he was going to say anything at all. Colour faded from her cheeks and desolation surrounded her.

It was soul-deep and wearying.

'This marriage is crazy,' she whispered.

And it seemed to rouse him. Matteo's eyes sparked with hers, and his jaw clenched, determination vibrating from him to Skye in passion-filled waves. 'Perhaps. But we *are* married, Skye. And I have no intention of letting you go.' He reached for her hand and caught it, bringing it to his lips. 'Come. Let me take you home. You said you are tired.'

She was.

Weary. Tired. Exhausted…but it was not the kind of exhaustion that could be cured with a rest. This state of weariness came from deep within, sapping her of all her strength.

'Yes,' she murmured. 'Fine. Let's go home.'

Matteo stared out at the canal without seeing. The moon was obstructed by thick, silver clouds and the city was almost completely dark. Only the far away glow of cruise ships offered any break in the bleakness of the night.

Skye was asleep upstairs, and Matteo remained where he was, looking out of the window as though answers might leap through it directly at him.

She was miserable, and that was his fault. The whole damned thing.

When had he decided that he would take the hotel? When had their marriage become a part of it?

Why hadn't he spoken to her? For surely, as soon as they'd made love, he had been confident Skye would have done almost anything he'd asked of her. But if she'd said no?

Then she'd have said no, he thought angrily.

When had he picked up the mantle of this feud as though his own life depended on it? Hadn't enough already been sacrificed to its purposeless pursuit? His grandfather had been broken by another man's vengeance.

And now Matteo was breaking Skye.

Had broken her.

Her face, as it had been that afternoon, came to his mind and he felt the sharp, unrelenting point of blame stab him square in the chest. She had looked...

Words flew through his mind. Sad? No, so much worse than sad.

Disappointed? Angry? Bereft?

All of the above. And something else. Something indefinable that sat heavily inside him like an accusation he would never lose.

Loving Maria had been simple. They'd made sense. She was a glamorous actress, albeit not a very good one, with legs that went on for ever. She had a penchant for expensive jewellery and six-star vacations, and he'd been happy to give them to her.

The fact she'd been using him for his social status had never occurred to him until she'd leap-frogged him to sleep with a Swedish duke. It had broken his heart. He'd felt that pain, which was how he recognised it so clearly on Skye's features.

He'd broken her heart. Badly. She had been a means to an end—a pawn in his fight to return Il Grande Fortuna to its rightful owner. He hadn't thought beyond the steps he needed to take to re-acquire the property. Marry Skye, make her trust him, take what he wanted.

And her?

Had he really never thought about how his actions might affect her? Or had he simply never cared, because she was the daughter of the only person he'd ever hated? Had he carried his hatred of Carey Johnson onto Skye, almost delighting in the knowledge he was using her?

With an angry sigh, he pushed to standing, moving towards the open doors and breathing in the unique tang of Venice's air.

He had only seen his grandfather cry once.

The sight had dug right into his heart and pressed into his nerves, changing everything he thought he knew about life. Alfonso hadn't known that Matteo had been watching. He'd thought he was alone. And he'd given into the groundswell of emotions without hesitation. They had consumed him, his strong, powerful body racked by sobs as he'd stared at the papers before him. Papers that hadn't made sense to Matteo at the time.

Now he knew what they were.

Overdue notices.

Mortgage payment requests.

Bills that Alfonso couldn't cover.

Matteo gripped the railing hard, remembering more than Alfonso's tears. Now he remembered Skye's father. The smug, condescending glint in his face as he'd refused to deal with Matteo. When he'd refused to see reason and sell the hotel back.

You're going to regret this. That was what Matteo had said.

It had been a prophetic statement, in the end. Only it was Matteo who was full of regrets.

Matteo who had lived to wish things—everything—had been different.

There was only one thing in the midst of this that made sense. There was one way Matteo had to erase Skye's hurts—and mitigate his own. There was one thing he could remind her of that would bring happiness to both of them.

His face was set in a grim line as he moved back into the villa, walking with a slow determination to her bedroom.

She was his wife. And, when she was in his arms, nothing else seemed to matter a damn.

CHAPTER TEN

IT WAS THE lawyer's office, right beside the doctor's, that made her think of it. Skye stared at her bruschetta without attempting to bite into it.

'Matteo?'

He, apparently, was suffering from no such lack of appetite. Skye watched as he forked a scoop of spaghetti into his mouth, savouring the flavours with obvious pleasure. 'Do you think perhaps we should speak to a lawyer?'

He froze, his eyes haunted as they met hers. *'Che?'*

'Everything between us is so complicated.' A line formed between her brows as she frowned, and anxiety swirled through her. Her pregnancy was still in its infancy, but before they knew it the baby would be with them. They'd be parents. 'Don't you think we should make arrangements now? Before we get too caught up in the whole "being a family" thing?'

'What kind of arrangements?' Neither his voice nor his expression gave anything away.

'Oh.' Skye waved a hand through the air and her selection of colourful bangles made a tingling noise as they knocked together. 'Everything.' Her frown deepened. 'I suppose a proper pre-nuptial agreement.'

Matteo returned his attention to the spaghetti, forking another generous portion into his mouth. 'We are married. A pre-nuptial agreement now would seem irrelevant.'

Skye nodded slowly, but her frame of mind didn't shift. 'I think we need to be pragmatic.' She swallowed. 'Do you remember what you said?'

He pulled a face, one of amusement and mockery. 'When?'

'You told me that you never lied to me.' She stared down at her plate, the past swirling like angry floodwaters. 'And you did. Not directly, but by omission. You knew how I felt, and how I believed you felt, and you didn't tell me the truth about any of this. But you never claimed to love me. You don't love me.' She paused, just long enough for him to interject. To say something that would ease the pain in her splintered heart.

He didn't.

She swallowed and pushed on. 'And I don't love you.' The words tasted bitter in her mouth. 'We need to remember that. Once the baby comes along and we love our child to the ends of the earth, I don't want to make the mistake of feeling like this is a real relationship.'

'It *is* a real relationship,' he said with exasperation. 'You are my wife in every way.'

'No.' Her eyes were enormous as they lifted to his. 'And it's not your fault that you don't realise that. You and I just have very different ideas of what a marriage is.' Her smile was lopsided. 'Ironic, really, given that you were the one who taught me to believe in fairy tales. Perhaps the reason you believe in them is that you expect so little of them.'

His eyes narrowed.

'I want it all. I want love and happiness and a true meeting of the minds. That will never be us.' She expelled a soft sigh. 'But we both want this baby, and so we'll raise it together. But I think it's very important that we don't lose sight of the truth of what we are.'

'And what's that, *bella*?'

'Well…' She pressed a single finger into the table top, tilting her head to the side as she examined her words carefully. 'We're two people who are going to have a baby. And we happen to be sleeping together.'

'Oh, good. I'm glad that's part of your contract.' He winked, his light-heartedness annoying her.

'I'm serious, Teo.' She tapped her finger once more. 'We both have considerable assets. I think we should get everything ordered. And I think we should have a custody arrangement drawn up. Just in case.'

'Hell, Skye. A *custody* arrangement? You're

pregnant with my child and you're already planning for a divorce?'

'Not necessarily,' she responded softly. 'But if we find this impossible, I don't want to have to go through all that then. I think we should rationally make a plan now, knowing that there's a good chance this won't work out. I think we should agree now, while we are level-headed and still… like one another enough to speak fairly.'

Matteo shook his head. 'No.'

'It makes sense.' She leaned forward. 'You know that. You're thinking with your heart, not your head.'

'I thought I didn't have a heart?'

'You do where our baby is concerned. You do where your *nonno* was concerned.' *It's only me you don't love*, Skye thought bitterly, reaching for her mineral water and sipping it to bring relief to her dry mouth. 'You told me yourself that you would fight for this baby. That you would stop at nothing to raise it. Well, I don't want to fight you later.'

'You'd rather fight me now?'

A muscle jerked in Skye's jaw as she clenched her teeth together. 'I'd rather not fight you at all. It's not ideal that we're going to be raising this child together, but I think we can make it work so long as we're reasonable. *I'm* prepared to be reasonable.'

'How so?' he prompted, dark colour staining his cheeks.

Fascinated at why he was so angry, Skye continued, 'Well, I'll stay in Venice. Near you. My business interests are well looked after. I don't need to be in London. And I can skip over when I do have to be on hand.' Emboldened by his silence, she continued, 'But I don't think we should share custody equally. I think the baby should have a home, somewhere they spend most of their time...'

'I agree completely.'

'And that it should be with his mother. With me.'

'Ah.' He shook his head. 'No. My child is being raised in my home.'

'Damn it, Matteo.' Skye leaned forward. 'I'm not saying we're going to get divorced. I'm just saying we should have a plan in place *in case*.'

'And I am saying I'm not prepared to discuss it,' he dismissed. 'Not now. Not ever. You are my wife. This is my child. We are a family.'

A family.

Skye froze, her face paling visibly.

A family?

All her life, it was the one thing she'd ever wanted, and this was not what she had expected it to look like. Nothing about what they were was what she'd imagined.

She swept her eyes closed, rejecting the description instantly.

'We're not family. We're just two people stupid enough to get pregnant when they should have known better.' She pushed her plate away. 'I'm not hungry.'

'Hey, hey.' He reached for her hand, curving his fingers over it. His surprise was obvious. Skye felt it too. She wasn't sure where her feelings were coming from, only that they were strong and they were real. 'This is good news. We both want this baby, don't we?'

She nodded, but her heart was heavy. She did, she wanted this baby so badly, but not like this. It was at such odds with how she'd imagined it would be. She pulled her hand away, clasping it in her lap, withdrawing from him in every way.

'But wanting the baby isn't the same as being a family. We're not a family. We're not even really a couple.' She swallowed. 'We both need to remember that.'

Matteo stared at her long and hard, his expression inscrutable.

A chasm of loss was swarming through him. But what could he say? How could he dispute her words? He had agreed to divorce her, when she'd come to Venice. Had he really been prepared to let her walk away?

Never to see her again?

The idea sat inside him like a strange kind of blade, running the sharpness of its edge through his body, his organs; tormenting him and wounding him in ways he was unable to appraise. But what could he say to her?

The reassurances he wanted to offer were buried deep inside him. It was only in bed that things made sense. There he could make her understand.

Unless...

The idea came to him out of nowhere, but instantly it was perfect.

'Skye? There is something I would like you to see.'

It was only once they'd boarded the flight to Rome that Skye twigged as to where he was taking her.

And what to see.

The hotel.

Anxiety had met tension in her gut, but now she felt an overwhelming sense of fascination. This was the building, after all, that had formed battle lines between her husband and her father.

And it was a beautiful building. At least, it would have been at one time. Now it was in a state of complete disrepair, the once-grand foyer boarded over so that even the high ceilings and marbled floor couldn't counteract the doom and gloom. But she knew what it was, even without his explanation. There were no signs out the front, there was no name on the door, but there was an air of importance that shrouded them as Matteo inserted a thick bronze key into the door and then scraped it inwards.

Pigeons had at some point taken up residence above, so that the step was covered in white splodges of poop, and there were empty soda cans discarded to the side of the door.

Matteo turned to face Skye with a raised brow. 'Your father never bothered to change the locks.' It was an indictment, as though the oversight was evidence that Carey hadn't cared about the building at all.

Inside, it was dark and enormous, and there was a lingering odour of dust and disuse.

'The last time I was here,' Matteo said thickly, 'It was just before Christmas. A tree stood over there.' He nodded towards the stairs, which were wide and sweeping, moving in a large, wide circle upwards to the mezzanine above. 'It had the most beautiful decorations, fine gold and a dark red, made of glass from Murano. It was a real tree, and enormous, so that the whole room smelled of pine. There were lights, twinkling little fairy lights that shimmered in the tree and across the ceiling. And there was a pianist in the corner, playing old-fashioned Christmas carols.' His eyes held some of the magic of the scene when they dropped to Skye's face. 'It was a special place, Skye.'

She nodded, perfectly able to envisage the beauty he had seen. The spectre of what he'd described. He crouched down, his trousers straining across his powerful haunches as he ran his fingertips over the floor. Snakes appeared in the thick coating of dust, revealing the grain of the marble beneath. 'This was quarried from the south and it took six months to ship it all up.' He stood, wiping his hands together, his eyes simply skimming over hers as he moved deeper into the hotel.

He moved to what Skye presumed would have been the reception area. A tall, dark wood bench with a marble top, the same as the floor. There were old-fashioned lights above it, as she'd imagined might have been used in banks in the twenties and thirties. Matteo pressed one of the gold switches on the wall but it did nothing.

Of course, there was no power.

'My great-great-great-grandfather built this hotel.' His voice carried an emotional note. 'He built it, and then each generation added to it. Yes, we created an empire, and yes, we have money, but this hotel—' He broke off, looking around the room with such helplessness that Skye's heart thudded inside her and pain gulfed in her belly. 'My family lives in these walls.'

She nodded and turned away from Matteo, unable and unwilling to expose herself to him in that moment, as realisation after realisation dropped through her. This place meant everything to Matteo, and her father had taken it and refused to sell it back.

'Your father didn't want it.' Matteo echoed her thoughts unconsciously. 'In fact, letting it fall into disrepair pleased him.' The words were uttered grimly.

'I don't believe it,' Skye said quietly. 'What reason could he have for buying something and then destroying it?'

'You know the answer to that.'

'Revenge,' she muttered, the word coursing through her venomously. 'Damned revenge.'

'Yes. He closed the hotel and had it boarded up as soon as it had been transferred to him. He told me he would have torn it down if the place weren't protected by historical covenants.'

'God, Matteo.' Skye squeezed her eyes shut, guilt filling her. 'I'm sorry.'

'This was not your doing, *cara*.'

'But he hurt you and I wish… I wish…'

'Hush.' Matteo came around from behind the reception desk, staring down at his wife and fighting every urge he had to touch her, knowing that it would solve nothing. 'You and I wish the same thing,' he said with frustration and urgency. 'We both wish it hadn't happened. But then…' He dropped his hands to her stomach, pressing his fingers into her, imagining the baby that was coming to life with every day that passed. 'We wouldn't have this gift. And I believe our baby is a gift, *cara*. I married you for the hotel, and it no longer matters. Not compared to the baby that grows within your body.' He dropped his mouth to hers, kissing her lightly. 'It means everything to me.'

Skye's heart trembled in her chest. His love for their unborn child filled her with happiness, but there was envy too, for the way he was able to be so lavish in his praise for the baby and remain as closed off to her as ever before.

'I know this is not as either of us would have wanted,' he continued thickly. 'But you are pregnant, and we need to focus on making this work. We do not know what will happen tomorrow, or next week, or in a month. But I am committed to this baby. With all that I am.'

Skye couldn't answer. Tears were clogged in her throat. She was a tangle of emotions; they were running through her, violent and insistent. She did her best to blank them. To be calm.

'I'm just trying to be smart.'

Matteo grinned. A grin that made her tummy flop and her own lips twist in an answering smile.

'You're already smart.' He shrugged. 'Why don't we try to be happy now?'

Happy. The word lodged inside her as he moved away once more, deeper into the hotel, towards the stairs. The smell was stronger there, and she realised that the carpet had been saturated over time. With a frown, she looked up and saw that the roof had a hole in it. It had been patched at some point, but a hint of the sky was visible through it.

Matteo was looking at it too, his expression impossible to read. Then he roused himself and took a step upwards, placing a hand in the small of her back. It was just a tiny gesture; it meant nothing. And, in terms of their intimacy, it was nothing like what they'd shared.

And yet it set Skye's pulse racing.

'How many rooms are there?' she asked, the question a little breathy as she tried to control her raging emotions.

If he noticed, he was sympathetic enough to respond in kind. 'There were fifty.'

'An even fifty?' she responded.

'Originally only twenty,' he said with a nod. 'When the trend was for accommodation to feature apartments rather than rooms. But over the time each lodging was downsized, to make more accommodation. Though, compared to a lot of hotels I've stayed in, they're still pretty spacious.'

'It's in a great location,' she murmured, moving up the stairs beside him. The hotel was just past The Vatican, overlooking the river Tiber.

'Yes.' Pride coloured the word. 'Once upon a time, this was the premier hotel in Rome. Royalty stayed here. Celebrities. Film stars. Musicians. Even a magician, for a time, who took to making red roses appear throughout the restaurant.' He was back in time, Skye could tell. The look on his face was one of nostalgia and grief. 'But it was more than that. The same families would come and stay at the same times each year. Groups would visit for Christmas, and again in the spring. It was a community. The breakfast room was alive each morning, and we always had the most incredible chefs. The food was truly *Romano*. Seasonal, fresh, exquisite.'

He expelled an angry breath, at odds with the wonderment his words were painting around them.

'Did you spend much time here?'

'As a child, *si*. My parents would bring us here every Christmas. We would sing carols in the foyer, and my *nonno* arranged a gift for every child in the hotel. I got to dress up as an elf and hand them out when I was very young.'

'You? An elf?' She looked at him quizzically, trying to imagine this specimen of pure masculinity as something so cute and harmless.

'Yes. What's wrong with that?'

'I'm just finding it hard to picture,' she said with a teasing smile. 'And after your parents died?' she pushed, wanting to know more, suddenly needing to understand her husband. So much of him was a mystery to her, and she didn't want that.

'Yes. For the few years my grandfather continued to hold the hotel. It was one of his last assets to go. Its loss destroyed him.'

She shook her head from side to side. 'And you were so young.'

'I swore that day that I would get the hotel back.' He stared around the foyer. 'I know it is just a building to you, but to our family, to me, this hotel is redemption.'

She nodded slowly, tears close to the surface.

'Let me show you the terrace.'

Skye went with him even though a part of her was dreading what was to follow.

The hotel was beautiful.

She got it.

Her family had taken it from his, and he had been angry about it. So angry that he'd married her to get it back.

The truth of that was appalling and yet, walking beside him through the hotel that her father had vandalised with his neglect, a hotel that her father had let fall into a state of complete abandon and disgrace, churned her up with anger.

She could imagine her husband's emotions. The strength of despair that must have filled him.

'He should have sold it back to you.'

'*Si, certamente,*' Matteo agreed. 'But he felt my father had taken everything from him. This was the perfect recompense for that.'

'People aren't objects,' Skye said with a shake of her head. 'Your mother chose to be with your father. If she'd loved my dad then she would have married him.' She paused, lifting a hand to her temple as a sharp pain burst through her.

Matteo noticed instantly. 'You are okay?'

'Yes, I'm fine.' She nodded. The pain passed and she continued upwards. 'These are bedrooms?'

'Now they are simply empty rooms.' The joke fell flat as remorse overrode humour. His eyes met hers for a moment before continuing an inspection of the run-down visage. 'The furniture was sold by the bank at auction to cover my grandfather's business debts.'

Skye nodded, pausing near one of the doorways. She lifted a hand to it, surprised when it pushed inwards. The room was large and spacious, open-plan, so that she could see the view of Rome from the grimy windows, and a bathroom that, at one time, would have been palatial.

A movement in the corner startled her and she squealed, but Matteo was right there, a strong arm around her waist. His smile was teasing. 'It is just a bat.'

'How do you know?'

His eyes scanned the room. 'They are everywhere in here. The security team I employ keeps drifters and vandals from setting up in the hotel, but bats we are powerless to prevent.'

Skye's heart turned over. 'You have security looking after the place? Even when it's no longer yours?'

'It will always be mine, in my heart,' he said seriously. 'If no one else is to look after it, then I will.' His smile was tight and didn't reach his eyes. 'I'm sure your father would have had me arrested for trespassing, if he were still alive.'

Skye said nothing. How could she deny it? It was obvious that the depth of her father's animosity had run deeper than she'd appreciated.

'I trust you will be kinder?' He winked, the smile on his face making her stomach flip and flop.

She nodded, distracted, and stepped out of the room, moving beside him back towards the stairs. Her headache had disappeared and now her head was throbbing instead, a low, dull pain. She pressed her fingers to her hair, loosening it and hoping the discomfort would pass.

She didn't want to cut their tour short.

'What is it?'

His solicitous question had Skye's head lifting towards his, and he was closer than she'd expected, so that she could have lifted up on tiptoes and kissed him. And she wanted to. She really wanted to.

Maybe it was the magic of the place but suddenly, though she was surrounded by the past, it no longer seemed to matter.

Let's be happy.

He was her happy.

But he was also her pain, her head pointed out.

'Skye?'

'Oh.' She nodded. 'Just a headache. I get them when I fly, sometimes.'

'Are you sure?'

'Yeah.' She nodded. 'I'll be fine. What next?'

CHAPTER ELEVEN

'I THINK WE should fix it.'

Matteo stared at Skye, pulling his attention away from the view of Rome to look at his wife. Here, finally, there was light. The rest of the hotel had fallen into a state of dinge and disrepair, but on the rooftop terrace he could imagine the hotel as it had once been.

Of course, back in its heyday, the terrace always had been full of Rome's elite sipping cocktails, overlooking the city, listening to the music that was playing.

'Fix what?'

'The hotel,' she murmured slowly. 'It's too beautiful, too grand, to be left like this.'

Matteo was very still, his eyes holding his wife's as though nothing made sense. 'You want to fix the hotel?'

'Yeah.' But his muted response made her doubt, made her pause. 'Don't you think it's a good idea?'

He pulled a face. 'Of course I do. It is what I intended to do when I…'

'When you stole it back from me, your unwitting wife?' She arched a brow meaningfully.

'As soon as I could,' he corrected. 'Skye…'

'It's okay.' Her response was soft. 'I get it. I understand why this place means so much to you.'

'Si?'

She nodded. ' I'll never forgive you for what you did. But I think my dad raised the stakes. I think he should have sold this place back to you. No, I think he should never have bought it.'

'We had to sell,' he said softly.

'But he bought it just to ruin it,' Skye murmured, shaking her head. 'Such needless destruction. I want to undo that.'

Matteo's eyes met hers and it was a moment that was perfect and poignant all at once. Because his eyes locked with Skye's and she felt, for the first time, as though maybe he did love her. And it wasn't about her at all. It was about the hotel. The damned hotel.

She looked away awkwardly. 'I know it will take time. And a lot of money. But can you imagine?'

'I don't need to imagine. I can remember.'

Skye nodded. 'I presume you have an idea as to where to start?'

His nod was brusque. 'Let's discuss it over dinner.'

Skye rolled her eyes. 'We ate on the plane.'

'Is our marriage going to consist of me suggesting food and you insisting you are not hungry? I do not seem to remember this being the case before.'

'Before, you found a way to deplete my energy and increase my appetite constantly.'

'Ah. Something I am happy to do now, believe me.'

Her stomach swooped and a wave of nausea buffered her. Suddenly, the idea of something like hot chips or focaccia was infinitely appealing. 'I could eat,' she said, changing the subject onto safer ground.

'And we will talk about Il Grande Fortuna.' His eyes glittered and her heart stuttered. He loved this place, and she owned it. He loved the baby she was growing. Suddenly, the fact he didn't love her seemed less important. Perhaps she could make do with these small crumbs?

She studied the hotel with renewed interest as they moved inside and down the stairs. While it was dark and dilapidated, so much of it was still glorious. The spine of the place was unmistakably perfect. The wide staircase, the chandeliers, the high ceilings and the skylights that were frosted over now with smog and dust but that had been, at one point, crystal-clear and had permitted light from the sun and the stars to filter into the hotel.

'It's beautiful,' she said as they reached the foyer, her eyes chasing the potential through the present.

'It was,' he agreed.

'And it will be again.' They walked towards the door in silence, but once there Skye paused. 'Thank you for showing it to me. It's helped me understand, I guess.'

'Understand?' he prompted.

'I understand why it means so much to you. If it had been less special…' She didn't finish the thought. She wasn't even sure of what she'd wanted to say.

Matteo pushed the door open and Skye stepped onto the street, looking left and right and imagining how they would rejuvenate even this aspect. She crossed to the other side as Matteo locked the door and stood with her hands on her hips, staring up at the façade, imagining it once it had been cleaned and had flags hanging from the brass poles that were languishing in neglect. She imagined it with window boxes that would be full of geraniums, all bright red, greeting the day as it rose overhead and offering their guests a hint of wild flora in the middle of Rome.

'What are you thinking of?' he asked as he came to stand beside her.

She smiled wistfully. 'Of the geraniums we'll have planted. On every window sill, just like at your villa.' She sighed. 'I loved waking up to them. Before. Before I left,' she clarified, colour darkening her cheeks at the oblique reference to their first attempt at married life. 'I used to pick them and place them in a vase—'

'I remember.' A gravelled interruption.

'I mean they're such an ordinary flower, I suppose, yet they're beautiful and resilient and so willing to grow,' she said with a shrug. 'I can see them here.'

'So can I,' he agreed, without taking his eyes from her face.

Discussing the hotel with Matteo over dinner brought the project more to life for Skye, so that by the time they boarded the flight home late that night, and then arrived back in Venice, Skye was full of excitement.

'I don't think I'm going to be able to sleep,' she murmured as they walked in the door of the villa. It was almost midnight, and she should have been exhausted, but a strange feeling was flooding her body.

The nausea was back, and she knew why. It was the sheer thrill of what they were going to do. Not just the baby, but everything else.

The hotel—something she'd viewed as an intense negative—was now something she contemplated with enthusiasm. And she was also utterly in love with it. Yes, she could admit her love for the hotel. It was simple. It was impossible *not* to love it. Or perhaps that was the baby in her stomach, willing her to connect with the ancestry that meant so much to the Vin Santos.

'We could swim instead,' he suggested with a sensual look that flopped Skye's stomach.

'Maybe a quick swim.' She nodded.

He reached down and held her hand, pulling her with him towards the stairs. She went willingly until they reached the terrace where they had first made love. The night of their wedding. And suddenly Skye didn't want to remember that. She didn't want to remember anything about their first attempt at marriage.

She wanted to write over the memories with new ones. Memories that were full of who she was now, the truth of their relationship something they both held in the palms of their hands. This was no love story, but there was enough between them to make this work. So long as she didn't forget. So long as she didn't lose her heart to him again.

'Matteo,' she murmured, and he stopped walking near the edge of the pool, pausing to look down at her. 'I want...'

She didn't finish the sentence. There was no need. He understood what his wife needed and wanted; it was the same desire that was heavy in his body. He dropped his mouth to hers, kissing her, holding her; bending her towards the ground and running his hands over her body at the same time, discarding her clothes, teasing her with the lightness of his touch while his mouth was ravaging hers.

He grabbed her hands and lifted them, pulling them behind his neck, and plying her body to his so there was barely even air between them. His dominance of her was almost as complete as hers of him. The moon shone overhead and the night was warm, yet Skye shivered in his arms, her body covered in a fine film of goose-bumps. He ran his hands down her back, finding the curve of her rear and lifting her effortlessly; wrapping her naked legs around his waist and holding her to his hard, confident body.

He turned slowly, kissing her neck, moving her to one of the sun lounges and laying her down with the kind of reverence that could make her forget everything.

Wasn't that what she'd wanted? To forget their first marriage and enter into this relationship as if it were new and fresh, and they were two different people?

And weren't they? She'd never again be the innocent, naïve woman who had believed herself swept off her feet.

Matteo didn't love her.

He never had.

Perhaps there was something smart in seeing their relationship as a transaction. Taking what was good from it and not lamenting what was missing.

There *was* so much good between them.

But could she ever really forgive him?

Did she want to?

His mouth drove into hers, sending all thoughts from her mind. But Skye was afraid. Afraid of how easily he could make her body sing. Afraid of how much she wanted him. Afraid of how she was going to cope in the years that would follow.

'This is just sex,' she whispered as he dragged his mouth to her breasts.

'Perfect can't-get-enough sex,' he agreed, with a smile that said nothing of the emotional torment she was feeling.

Would she never get enough? Was this a life sentence?

Her heart skidded inside her.

And it was joy that made her smile.

She'd never be able to resist him, and maybe that was okay. In that moment, everything was perfect. But it was a perfection that couldn't and wouldn't last. If only Skye had known to make the most of it while she could...

'Matteo?'

It was the middle of the night. No, it was past that. They'd made love somewhere in the early hours of the morning and then he'd carried Skye to his bed, insisting that she spend the night beside him. He couldn't have said why it mattered so much to him, only that he liked the way it felt to have her body curled back against his, for his arm to be wrapped around her stomach. To know that their baby was there, safe and loved.

He groaned, smiling as he pressed a kiss into Skye's warm, smooth shoulder. But it was damp, covered in salty perspiration, and the taste on his lips had him blinking his eyes open.

'Something's wrong,' she said with more urgency, and he focused on her face. She was sweating all over: her hair was wet, and she was pale and shaking.

'*Bella*, what is it?' He pushed out of bed and was reaching for his jeans in one movement. 'Skye?'

She pressed the palm of her hand to her stomach and tears filled her eyes. 'Something's *wrong*!' She said it with more urgency. 'I'm scared.'

It was awful.

Awful for him, but so much worse for his wife. All he could do was hold her hand and whisper to her in Italian as the proof of their loss slowly left her body. He kissed her and he held her, but Skye wasn't really in the room with him. She was stoic and brave, but she had obviously divorced her mind from the horror of what they were experiencing.

Her eyes were empty, just like her womb, just like her soul and her hopes for the future. The future they had both imagined and hoped for.

She listened to the doctor, who came to assure Skye that sometimes these things 'just happened'. She listened to the nurses as they kindly explained that lots of women miscarried early on in their pregnancies and later went on to have healthy babies. That she had an eighty percent likelihood of carrying to term 'next time'. She listened as her heart was breaking and her body was emptying itself of the life that she had loved with all her heart.

And only when they were alone, and an unappetising dinner had been brought with a sweet cup of tea, did tears moisten her eyes.

'*Cara*...' Matteo crouched beside her, trying to draw her eyes in his direction. But she stared at the wall with eyes that were wet and distraught. 'Talk to me.'

She couldn't.

There were no words.

She reached for her tea and sipped it, happy when the boiling water scalded her tongue. Pleased that the pain meant she was alive again. That she could feel.

Because inside she was numb.

She was cold, she was empty and she was alone in a way that was so much worse than any other form of loneliness she'd ever known.

The fluorescent light overhead flickered, and with each dimming it made a crackling sound. Just a low, muted buzzing. Skye heard it as though she were in a void.

A silent sob racked her body, lifting it off the bed and dropping it back down again. She turned away from him then, not wanting him to see the anguish that contorted her features.

'Bella, per favore...' He groaned, reaching a hand up and laying it on her thigh. She didn't pull away from him physically, but emotionally she was cutting every cord that had ever joined her to him. She was rejecting the intimacy and rejecting him, relegating him to a portion of her mind that was never to be looked at again.

'I want to go home,' she said after several long moments.

'Of course. I'm sure that will happen soon. They probably just want to observe you a little longer, to be sure you are okay.'

'Okay?' she repeated with soft disbelief. Then, she nodded. Because he seemed to expect it. 'I'm okay.' She placed the plastic tea cup onto the table beside her, staring at the ripples in the drink's surface.

Matteo's frown was infinitesimal and he smothered it quickly before she could see it. Not that she was looking in his direction. Her face was averted with unwavering determination.

God, her face.

She was so pale. He pushed up and sat on the bed beside her, wincing as she flinched away from him.

'Please.' It was just a whisper. Her fingers caught at the blanket, pulling at it awkwardly. 'I want to leave here.'

'Lo so, lo so.' He reached up and ran a hand gently over her hair; it was matted and still damp from the perspiration. 'I am sure it won't be long.'

She spun round to face him, dislodging his touch. 'I need you to get me out of here. Now.'

The urgency of her heart communicated itself through her words. He stood immediately. There was nothing he wouldn't do for her in that moment. 'I'm so sorry, Skye.'

'Sorry?' she whispered, her eyes enormous. 'Why are you sorry? This was my fault, not yours.'

He shook his head slowly. 'No. It wasn't anyone's fault. They told you that...'

'I want to go home,' she said with more urgency. 'Please.'

He nodded, a single, terse movement. 'I'll speak to someone.' His eyes clung to her as he moved to the door. 'Just wait. A moment.'

She didn't respond. What was she meant to do?

Did he expect her to get up and try to make a bid for freedom out of the air-conditioning vent?

There were no windows in the room.

No view of the outside. And somehow that felt appropriate, as though even the beauty of Venice had turned its back on her.

When Matteo came back a few minutes later, it was with a doctor clutching a chart. Her smile was sympathetic as she studied Skye.

'I'm happy to let you go home,' the doctor said without preamble. 'So long as you'll come back in a week, or at the first sign of any complications.'

'What kind of complications?' Matteo responded.

'Oh, infection. Raised temperature. Anything out of the ordinary. Okay?'

Skye bit down on her lip and nodded, though she was barely comprehending. 'Fine. Of course. Thank you.' The words sounded so normal, but *nothing* was normal. The whole world was off its axis.

'You will take care of her?'

'*Si.*' Matteo's single-word answer was gruff. Skye squeezed her eyes shut against it. One syllable, so full of falsity. So unnecessary.

'I'll be fine,' Skye murmured, attempting a smile. It felt awful on her lips, heavy and sodden all at once. She let it fall almost instantly.

The images she had allowed to populate her mind were disintegrating, like puffs of cloud she couldn't reach out and grab. She squeezed her eyes shut and tried to picture the baby she'd imagined them having. But he was gone. That chubby face wouldn't come to mind. She couldn't remember the dimples she'd seen there, nor the curls of dark hair.

She couldn't see him! She couldn't feel him!

Panic rose inside her, and then nausea, and she reached out instinctively. Matteo was there, his arms wrapping around her, holding her. He smelled so good, so strong, and he felt so right. But he was wrong. This was all wrong.

She stiffened and pushed away from him, swallowing away the pain in her throat. There would be a time to process this. For now, Skye was in survival mode.

A water taxi was waiting to take them home, and the boat operator was far cheerier than either Skye or Matteo had tolerance for. They sat in silence, shocked and uncomprehending as the boat steered them towards Matteo's home.

It was a clear, sunshine-filled morning.

Skye's heart felt only coldness.

When the boat came to a stop near Matteo's, he held a hand out for her, to help her step out. Only the fact she was still in pain and discomfort implored her to take it. Just for the briefest possible moment.

She didn't want to touch him.

She didn't want to *feel* his touch.

'Thank you,' she murmured, staring up at the

villa. The geraniums were smiling down at her, encouraging her.

She blinked away from them. She did her best to blot out the sunshine too.

'Come, *cara*.' He put a hand in the small of her back. She stepped forward, shaking him free, moving as quickly as she could towards his front door.

Everything was different.

Not like before, when she'd returned to their marriage and she'd thought herself miserable.

She was truly miserable now, and she viewed everything through the veil of that misery and despair.

It was still only early in the day, and they'd hardly slept. The last twenty-four hours passed before her eyes like some kind of movie. They'd been in Rome and she'd been so happy, looking at the hotel and imagining the way they could heal the wounds that had caused its demise. Had she hoped it might lead him to love her?

Yes.

She had felt that it was a beginning, when really it had been an end.

For what purpose did their marriage serve now? There was no love. And no baby.

And no point in her staying in Venice with Matteo.

CHAPTER TWELVE

'You must eat something.'

Skye didn't smile, though a part of her remembered the number of times he'd said just that to her. But then she'd been pregnant, and his concern had made sense. He'd been worried for their baby.

Now?

She shook her head. It wasn't his place to worry about her.

In the three days since the miscarriage, she'd survived on tea and dry biscuits, and she'd barely moved from her spot on the sofa. She stared out at Venice, but she wasn't really looking. She was simply existing.

'I'm not hungry,' she said, because Matteo seemed to be waiting for her to say something.

'But your body is recovering. You must be strong and well, Skye.'

'Why?' she asked, though it wasn't really a question, so much as a word that was breathed out by her sigh.

'Because. I need you to be well.'

Skye didn't look at him. She couldn't. 'Why?'

He crouched beside her and pressed a hand into her thigh. 'Because you are my wife.'

She flinched, as though he'd threatened her. 'No.'

Matteo was very quiet, watching her for several long seconds, and then he abandoned the conversation. Not out of a desire to avoid it, but out of a need to avoid upsetting her further. He could see her breath becoming rushed and her cheeks flushing pink. He let it go, for the moment. 'Would you like a tea?'

'No.' She turned to face him now. There was nothing familiar in Skye's face. She was altered and broken, completely different. He could hardly recognise the woman he'd married. Her face was pale and her hair was heavy and lank. Her eyes, though, were so full of darkness and aching sadness.

His chest squeezed, as though it had been weighed down with something heavy.

'If you have the papers redrawn, I'll sign the hotel over to you before I leave.'

Matteo froze, his body tense, his expression incomprehensible. 'Before you leave? Where are you planning to go, Skye?'

She turned away from him again, staring out at Venice. It was annoyingly perfect beyond the window. Sunny and bright, with blue skies as far as she could see. 'Home. I want to go home.'

His tone had urgency. 'You *are* home.'

She swallowed, her throat moving visibly. 'No.'

'We're married and we live—'

She spoke over him. 'Without the baby, there's no point to my being here.'

'Yes, there is!' He was emphatic. 'My God, Skye. This doesn't change anything. It's…it is all the more reason for you to stay. I want to… You can't leave. I want us to be together. I want to have a family with you, Skye, one day. This wasn't the right time. This wasn't meant to be. But that doesn't mean we can't have other babies one day—'

'Don't!' The word was a sharp hiss and she recoiled as she said it. Recoiled from him and his words, from each and every platitude designed to make her feel better but which had the exact opposite effect. 'God, just don't.'

'Cara,' he said softly. 'You are hurting. So am I. It will take time before we feel like ourselves again…'

'You have no idea what I'm feeling,' she said, tilting her head to his. 'So don't tell me how I'm supposed to act. Don't tell me I'm going to be like myself again.'

He nodded sympathetically, but when he spoke it was with grim determination. 'This was my baby too. Do you think you are the only one who is grieving?'

She sucked in a deep breath. 'Are you trying to make me feel guilty now?'

He sighed. 'No, nothing like that. But you are not alone in this.'

'Yes, I am.' She squeezed her eyes shut against all the pain and sadness that was choking her. 'And I *want* to be alone.' She lay back against the sofa, turning her back on him and closing her eyes.

She breathed in and out and now, with her eyes shut, and sadness filling her up; she could finally see their baby again. She could see his little face and the dimples she'd imagined he'd have; she sobbed freely, believing herself to be alone. She sobbed with all the grief in her heart. And she wasn't just grieving their baby. It was everything. The loss of hope. Of love. Of her belief that she had found her own *happily ever after.*

'You're not alone,' he said finally, after so long that she'd presumed he'd left. 'I'm here with you.'

She sobbed harder, grieving their baby as well as their love. Grieving the life she'd imagined before her.

It was all a lie, just like everything about them.

'I wish I'd never met you. I wish you'd never spoken to me.'

'Hush, hush,' he murmured, patting her back.

'I hate you,' she sobbed into the pillow. 'I hate you so much.'

Skye wasn't sleeping, so much as dozing fitfully. She was exhausted, yet the second she closed her eyes and drifted off she awoke in a panic, feeling as though she were drowning and there was nothing she could do to stop the water that was gushing into her lungs.

She woke in such a manner early the next day, and she noticed three things.

A small water glass had been filled with geraniums at some point and placed on the occasional table beside her. And she knew who had done it. The gesture iced her heart, for it was at once both so sweet and meaningless.

Matteo was asleep across the room, sitting in an armchair dressed in day clothes, looking as exhausted as she felt.

And she was hungry.

It was just a kernel of need, but it was unmistakable. She pushed off the sofa quietly, careful not to wake Matteo, and padded into the kitchen. There was no Melania, no one. Skye wondered, vaguely, if Matteo had told Melania. Had even asked her to give them space.

The fridge was full, as always, but when Skye opened it and looked inside she couldn't make up her mind as to what she felt like.

She opted for a small croissant, simply because she could eat it without any preparation or fuss. She took it with her onto the terrace and stared out at the city, her stomach dropping with grief at this place that would never be her home.

'Cara.' The word was gravelled. She spun

around, her cheeks flushing with something like guilt. Matteo looked…terrible and delicious all at once. She tamped down on the stirring of primal needs.

She wouldn't answer their call ever again.

'I thought you were gone.'

She blinked, turning away from him, facing out towards Venice. 'No.'

She felt him move behind her and braced for the inevitable physical contact. Perhaps understanding what she needed most of all, he stayed a little distance away, giving her space.

'How are you feeling today?'

She shrugged. What words were there for how she felt?

'Come and rest some more,' he said softly. 'It's early.'

She nodded, but didn't move. 'I don't understand,' she said finally. 'I don't understand what happened.'

His throat moved as he swallowed. She caught the action and wondered at his own emotions. 'The doctor said that, more than likely, there was a genetic abnormality within the baby. An "incompatibility with life", she called it.'

Skye squeezed her eyes shut, the detail layering more guilt onto her wounded heart.

'There was nothing you could have done differently.'

'Of course there is. It was my baby. My body. I should have…'

'There was nothing you could have done.' He was insistent.

'Do you know what I thought? Only a week or so ago? I told you that I wished I was having the baby with anyone but you.' Her voice cracked. 'What I meant was that I wished I wasn't pregnant with your baby.'

She let the words hit their mark, strangely pleased when his face paled beneath his tan and his eyes squeezed shut for a moment.

'I wished I wasn't pregnant, and now I'm not.'

'One thing has nothing to do with the other,' he said after a moment, the words gentle.

'I didn't deserve the baby.' A hollow whisper. 'That's why I lost it.'

'No, stop. You must stop.' He drew his brows together, his expression sombre. 'Do not torment yourself with what you should and could have done differently.' His mouth was a grim slash. 'If either of us was at fault here, if either of us should have behaved differently, it was not you.'

He turned his attention back to the canal. 'I am sorry, Skye. For everything I've done to you.' She jerked her head around to face him, shock making the details of his appearance somehow brighter than they should have been. The grey flesh beneath his eyes; the stubble on his chin that spoke of a lack of interest in grooming, the way his mouth was drawn downward.

Her heart ached for him.

And for herself.

And for their baby.

'I'm going inside,' she murmured, turning and moving back into the villa.

A week after the loss, Skye was no longer in any physical discomfort. Her body was itself again. But her mind and heart would never be the same. She woke early one morning and went to the terrace, diving into the water of the pool wearing only her underwear. She swum for an hour, up and back, up and back, hoping that she would exhaust herself to the point of sleep finally. Real sleep, not sleep tormented by dreams of what their baby might have been like, and the certainty that she'd lost something she'd never replace.

A week after that, and she had learned to numb herself to the grief. At least, some of the time.

And she had accepted that she had to move on.

All the while, Matteo had watched her, had been close to her without invading her space, had accepted her state of non-communication and had waited for the time when she would open up to him again.

His waiting was futile, though, because she never would.

Later that night, once Melania had set the table for dinner, Skye poured herself a large glass of Pinot Grigio. She sipped almost half of it, placed it at her setting at the table, and went in search of Matteo.

When she found him, her heart almost cracked open once more.

He was in his study, holding the stupid stuffed toy he'd bought for the baby.

The ground lurched beneath Skye and it took every ounce of strength she had been trying to rediscover not to break down in tears.

'I've booked a taxi,' she murmured. 'It will be here soon. I thought we could discuss the logistics of our divorce before I go.'

God, the words had sounded so clinical and professional when she'd rehearsed them, but now they just seemed discordant and wrong.

His eyes, hollow and almost looking suspiciously moist, lifted to hers. 'Why?'

Skye didn't know if he was talking about the baby, or about her, or any of it. She shook her head, staring across at him, the cavern of the room opening before her.

She smiled, a weak smile that was almost impossible to unearth. 'I don't belong here. I want to go home.'

'You're my wife.'

Skye ignored the statement. He'd said it often

enough, and she knew that the words meant nothing. 'Only until our divorce is processed.' She swallowed past the pain in her throat. 'We lost the baby, Teo.' She said it as though perhaps he hadn't realised. 'There is nothing left here.'

He moved quickly, sweeping across the room, dropping the toy as he went. 'Yes, there is!' He spoke with urgency. 'There's us. You and me.'

She shook her head. 'No.'

'I don't want you to go. I need you…'

Skye swept her eyes shut; her heart was twisting painfully in her chest, despite her certainty that she had no more grief left to feel. 'Why? Why do you need me?'

'Why do you need me?' he pushed, lifting a hand to her chest, feeling her heart beating, feeling her goodness.

Because she loved him.

Because he was a part of her.

She stiffened her spine, mentally holding herself at a distance from him. 'I don't.' And she didn't want to. 'I need to start forgetting.'

'Please, don't.' He lifted his hands to cup her face, and she saw all the grief he was feeling. She felt guilt for it. For the baby she'd offered him and then lost. 'Don't forget.'

'Why not?' She sniffed, focusing on a point over his shoulder. 'I look at you and I just remember…everything. I don't want to remember.' She cleared her throat. 'I don't want any payment for the hotel. It should never have been taken from you.' She reached up and cupped her hand over his, allowing herself to be weak for a moment. She closed her eyes and breathed him in. 'When it's finished, I might come back and stay in it for a night.'

It was something she had no intention of doing, though. When she left, she would never again set foot in Italy.

'This is madness. You are grieving now, we both are, but that doesn't change anything about our marriage. Even before I knew about the baby I didn't want you to go. You are my wife and you love me.'

Skye shivered softly. Was there any point in denying it? To him, to herself? She did love him. It was an incontrovertible fact. 'You don't love me, though.' She looked up at him. 'Do you?'

He stared down at her, and for a moment she thought he was actually going to say it. She wondered how it would sound, to hear those words on his lips and know they were meant for her. But then he turned away from her and scooped the toy up off the floor.

'You mean more to me than any other woman ever has.'

Skye's lips twisted at the faint praise. 'Let's talk in the dining room,' she said quietly.

'A last supper?' he queried, turning around to pin her with his gaze.

'It is better that we sort out the logistics now. So that we don't need...'

'To speak again?' He swore under his breath. 'I don't want that! I don't want you to go!'

'I can't stay.' She spun away from him and stalked down the corridor away from him, her heart breaking, her anger rising, her feelings rioting. He was just behind her, reaching for her, pulling at her hand so that she stopped and collided with him.

'Why not?' He was right there, his chest moving hard and fast as he sucked in air and expelled it angrily.

'Because there's no baby! And no love. This marriage is just a cruel joke.'

'I know nothing of love,' he said, the words rasping inside him. 'The one time I thought I felt it I was so wrong. I know nothing about how hearts are meant to feel. And I am so sick of hearing people talk about a heart as though it is the beginning and end of what a man is supposed to give to a woman! Do I love you? Do you have my *heart*?' He stared at her and she held her breath, her eyes clinging to his.

'No, *cara*. You have *all* of me. My blood. My body. My mind. All of me is yours, and has been since the moment I met you. When I tell you I need you, I do not mean it in the way you think. It is not sex that I am referring to. I *need* you as I *need* air, and I *need* water. You are no less important to me and my survival than these things. I thought I married you for the hotel.' He lifted a finger to her lips, silencing anything she might be going to say. 'But somewhere in those early days, while you were falling in love with me, I was doing the exact same thing.'

His words ripped through her; they were everything she'd needed to hear a fortnight earlier. Now, they only compounded her grief. 'Don't say that! You don't need to lie to me, Matteo! You can have the hotel. You can let me go. You can get on with your own life...'

'*You* are my life! Yes, I wanted the hotel. I spent so much of my life wanting it that I did whatever I could to finally have it. But that changes *niente* about what I want now.' He cupped her face, holding her still so that he could stare down at her, his eyes boring into hers.

'How can you not see what you are to me? Why do you need me to define how I feel about you by the way other people feel? Nothing about what we are has ever been experienced before. Do you truly believe this is just love? Such an insipid, boring, common description for what I feel! I despise that word, as though saying it changes a damned thing! Love is a feeling that can be transient and cheap, that many claim to have felt. The word is thrown about like emotional confetti. That's not what we are! No one has felt this! Ever! I have told another woman that I loved her, and yet I never felt for her what I do for you! It cheapens what we are, to use that same word. You are my *everything*. You are like a universe that lives in my chest. Is this what you need to hear?'

She stared at him and could scarcely breathe for the flood of feelings rioting inside of her. 'You have never, not once, told me any of that. How can I believe you truly mean it? I'd be stupid to trust you again.'

'Believe me, *cara*, I would have told you sooner if I had understood my own feelings.' His face was pale, and she didn't doubt the truth of what he was saying. 'I did marry you for the hotel. I didn't care about you, or what you wanted. Not at first. I can't tell you when that changed. I only know that, now? Now you are *all* I care about.' He shook his head angrily. '*Dio*, when you talked about a pre-emptive custody arrangement the other day, I felt like you were bludgeoning me. Even then, I didn't understand why I should have such an irrational response to your very logical suggestion. But I see now, Skye. I have been so in love with you this whole damned time that the idea of losing you again was impossible. Impossible.'

He stared at her for a long moment. 'The first

time you left, I was so angry. I was angry because I didn't want to feel anything else. And when you came back, you wanted a divorce, and I thought I should give it to you. I see now that I signed the papers out of shame and guilt, out of a wish to undo the pain I had caused you. Out of a need for you to be happy, because I loved you. Because I loved you with all my heart.'

Skye shook her head, instinctively railing against his version of events that didn't fit with how she'd felt.

His voice became more urgent, as he felt her pulling away from him despite everything he was offering. 'And we were given a baby. A reason to *fight*. To fight for what we have.'

'But the baby is gone…'

'Yes.' Emotions passed over his face. 'And we will grieve that loss for ever. For the rest of our lives. But we will grieve *together*, because we are meant to be so.'

Oh, but her heart. The heart he held, the heart he'd broken, the heart that was now ripped into tiny pieces, the heart that was empty. It rejected everything he said. It had learned, at last.

'You were right,' she whispered, pulling back, away from his touch, standing straight. 'Love is a lie. It's all a lie.' She forced herself to meet his eyes. 'I can't stay.'

He squared his strong jaw, his eyes warring

with hers, his natural tendency to overrule and dominate combated by his newly discovered need to comfort his wife. 'This isn't.'

She bit down on her lip. 'There's too much pain here.'

'But so much good,' he murmured.

'Not enough.' She blinked, stepping away from him. 'I have wanted love all my life, and I fell in love with someone who doesn't even know what it means.'

'I told you…'

She swallowed, trying to make sense of her thoughts. 'I know it wasn't just about the hotel. And I know it wasn't just about the baby.' Her voice cracked on the single word, as her dreams and hopes sped away from her. 'You don't like losing, Matteo. And if I walk out that door, you've lost.'

'I don't care about losing. I care about losing *you*!'

The distinction was an important one, but Skye was becoming more convinced of what she needed to do with every painful moment that passed.

'You've already lost me.' She blinked, but tears still filled her eyes. 'You lost me the day you proposed, knowing it was just for the hotel.' She lifted a hand, her trembling fingers running over his cheek. 'You lost me the day you stood in front of me and vowed to love me for the rest of your life, knowing you didn't feel that way. You lost me all the times you've told me that all we have is sex. You lost me a long time ago. I'm just making it official now.' She pulled away from him, her heart no longer breaking. It simply ceased to exist. 'I have to go.'

There was disbelief and desperation etched on his face. 'Give me a chance. Another week…'

'You need to understand, Matteo.' The words echoed with the strength of her intent. 'I don't *want* to give you a chance. I don't want you to change my mind. I don't ever want to trust you not to hurt me, because I know that you will. You're incapable of love, and love is all I really want.' She cleared her throat and rallied her emotions as best she could. 'I'd appreciate it if you'd pass my best onto Melania. Explain that I couldn't stay.'

Matteo's skin was pale beneath his tan. 'Skye, I do love you. With all that I am…'

Her eyes were defiant but her voice was soft. Gentle. 'It's okay. No more lies. You can let me go. Let's both pretend this never happened.'

CHAPTER THIRTEEN

SKYE STARED AT the flowers. She admired the lilies with their pristine white petals. *He says you are very soft. Like a petal.*

Instinctively, she looked away. Towards the daffodils with their bright-yellow colour so like the sunlight of Venice. Her heart lurched and her eyes skidded onwards.

'What'll it be, miss?'

She blinked at the man standing like a flower-worshipping troll deep in the cave of his floristry van and tried to smile. She suspected it came off as more of a wince, as most of her smiles had done for a while.

Her eyes dropped back to the collection of blooms.

The red gerberas were beautiful, but the second she looked at them she saw only the geraniums that had grown rampant at Matteo's villa, and she couldn't bear to have a substitute for the flower.

'Miss?'

She nodded and reached for a thick collection of gladioli, choosing them at random.

But, as she walked home and held them in the

palm of her hands, she had to acknowledge that their long, spiked stems somewhat matched her current mood. They were still barely budding. Just a streak of colour along the length indicated that, one day soon, they would be bright and glorious. For the moment, they were simply a beginning.

She moved through the streets of Fulham, weaving through people, breathing in as she past her favourite dim sum house, enjoying the intoxicating combination of soy sauce and spices that permeated the air.

It was a nice day, given that autumn was now upon them, and the local pub had people spilling out onto the footpath. Their noise was loud. She kept her head averted, refusing to look at the flower pots that had, yes, geraniums, but also pansies and stocks. But in twisting her face away, she looked across the street and saw...

Her heart thumped. She froze.

Matteo?

His back was to her, but he wore the navy suit she loved and his dark hair was brushing against its collar. Her tongue felt heavy in her mouth. Sweat beaded across her upper lip and she held her breath.

A woman emerged from the bakery, her smile wide. God, she was pregnant, her stomach rounded as though she were due to have the baby any moment. Skye's gut twisted. The man turned to embrace her and Skye saw his pale skin and slightly tipped nose.

It was not Matteo. She pushed her head down and hurried onwards, turning off the main road after a block and moving down the little side street on which her townhouse stood.

'Hi!' One of the little boys from the house next door called to her, his public school uniform in a state of disarray that Skye suspected would earn him a talking to when his mother and father got home. His tie was wonky and his shirt pocket was almost completely torn loose.

'Rugby,' he explained with a shrug, and she nodded, turning away and moving quickly towards her gate. She unclipped it and pushed up the stairs, unlocking her door and heaving it open as though it weighed a ton.

Simple tasks such as opening a door had become onerous since leaving Italy, but she knew that wouldn't last. One day she would feel like herself again.

Flowers would help.

Her house was dark and cold, despite the mildness of the day. She frowned as she moved deeper into it, stepping over the mail on the floor, resolving to tend to it later, as she had done for the last week or so.

She arranged the gladioli in a slender vase and

turned the television on, raising the volume until noise and conversation filled much of the downstairs of her home. She liked the company.

She liked that the television expected nothing of her.

The afternoon dragged.

She made a cup of tea at some point around dark.

And then a piece of toast nearer to nine.

And, finally, she decided she'd done enough. She'd made it through the day. She could sleep, and start all over again in the morning.

Her expression was grim, her skin pale like moonlight as she moved back through the house. Her eyes caught the stack of mail on the floor as she turned to move up the stairs.

With a resigned sigh, she changed course, crouching down and scooping it up.

It would make for bedtime reading at least, she thought, wishing she'd thought to pick up some new books while she'd been out. Maybe other people's lives would provide the distraction she needed.

She tossed it unceremoniously on the bed and began to undress for the shower.

The water was warm. She luxuriated beneath it, wiping her mind clean, refusing to think about Italy, about Matteo and about their baby. She refused to think about the things he'd said to her on her last afternoon in Venice.

But none the less, his words rolled through her, spinning around her and making her gasp.

'You are my everything. *You are like a universe that lives in my chest.'*

She moaned softly, reaching for the loofah and running it over her body.

'When I tell you I need you, I do not mean it in the way you think. It is not sex that I am referring to. I need *you as I* need *air, and I* need *water.'*

She had been right to leave him. She could never trust him, and what was love without trust?

Memories of their days walking through Venice flooded her—of his sharing his *gelato* with the little Romani boy, of the way he'd held her hand and talked about the history of the city and his time growing up in it—and she sobbed, unable to hold her heartache at bay a moment longer.

It was here, in the night time, alone in her enormous house, that she finally allowed herself to admit that the pain wasn't easing. That the ache inside her chest was growing wider with each day that passed. With each day she spent away from Matteo.

It was here that she always came to question her decision, even though she was certain, really, that she'd been right to leave him. To protect herself from the dangers of loving a man like Matteo and living in fear of when his favour would cease to exist.

She closed her eyes; she saw him and her heart lurched.

She banged her palm against the shower then dropped her hand to the taps, turning them slowly, easing the water. But she didn't get out. She stood there immobile for a time. Broken. Her head bent, her back bowed, her body emptying of any hope, happiness and light.

She would gain control of this, though.

She'd known loss and loneliness all her life, and she'd always found ways to cope. She would do so again. Wouldn't she?

In the end, she pushed the mail to one side of the bed and fell asleep naked, with no energy to so much as find a nightgown. Exhaustion was the saving grace of her current emotional state, but it was followed reliably by insomnia, so that somewhere before dawn she woke, bright and early, and she knew she wouldn't find the relief offered by sleep again.

She sat up in her bed and reached for the stack of mail, contemplating making a cup of coffee, and decided she'd reward herself with a mug only when she'd successfully made her way through at least five of the envelopes.

The first three were invitations to parties and

events. She pushed them to one side, knowing she needed to engage some kind of assistant to deal with this stuff. Usually, she was able to keep on top of it, but since Venice she'd been…well…a mess. Besides, she wasn't in a particularly festive mood.

The fourth item was an advertising flyer. She pushed it away without looking and reached for the fifth. It was a little thicker than the rest. She slid her finger under the glued back, already fantasising about the coffee she was going to be enjoying within minutes.

She unfolded the paper and instantly caught her breath.

Her fingertips shook as she straightened the page properly.

The Vin Santo business emblem was unmistakable. A powerful VS embossed in black. She ran her fingertip over it even as her eyes fled to the words.

They were handwritten.

It means nothing without you.

Her heart raced hard and fast against her chest. And, for the first time since leaving Venice, colour was in her cheeks and something like hope and joy filled her. She flipped the page and saw what was behind it.

The contracts she'd had sent for the transfer of the hotel.

Exactly as she'd sent them, except for one vital detail.

He'd put a large, black cross through each page. And had failed to add his signature.

She shuddered, falling back against the pillows, her eyes shut, the letter clutched to her chest.

It means nothing without you.

She groaned, pushing the bed linen off her and standing, reaching for her robe. She wrapped it around her body, cinching it at the waist, and brought the letter with her as she moved back downstairs into the kitchen.

She slid a pod into her coffee machine, pressing the button distractedly as she read his words for the tenth time.

It means nothing without you.

The hotel was all he'd wanted.

It was why he'd married her.

And she was offering it to him now with no strings, no regrets.

Did he really mean this? Why not just take the damned hotel and be done with it?

It means nothing without you.

She closed her eyes and she was back in Rome, staring at the building, admiring its beauty, imagining it for its potential. Seeing it as they would have made it, with its flowers, its flags and its doormen.

She breathed in and tasted the history of the

hotel, the past that lived within its walls. She saw it as Matteo had described, full of people and music, atmosphere and pleasure. She saw the terrace with elegant cocktails and guests milling about.

And she forced her eyes open.

For the first time in a month, she knew what she had to do.

This hotel had to be returned to its rightful owner. Matteo *had* to fix the damage her father's vengeance had done. From this pile of sadness, something good could come.

And she'd just have to make him see sense.

Matteo stared at the email with a strange sense of non-comprehension. Skye's lawyer was requesting a meeting, in person, with him.

And he knew what it was about.

The damned divorce.

In the five weeks since she'd left, he'd begun to hope that perhaps silence was golden. That she'd changed her mind. That perhaps she needed space to grieve, to come to terms with their loss, but she would see he'd meant every word he'd said.

He'd given her the breathing space to do what she needed; he owed her that much. And every day that had passed he'd hoped meant she would change her mind. That her certainty was fading.

But now?

He shook his head, reaching for his phone and dialling the number on the top of the page.

'Matteo Vin Santo. I need to make an appointment with Charles Younger.'

Skye stared at the view of London, wondering at her own treachery. She had always loved this city, yet now she found herself seeing only its grey sky and bleak steel monoliths. She didn't see the way the sun glinted off the side of the buildings, nor the way the Thames glistened through its heart like a powerful lifeblood.

She flicked her gaze down to her wristwatch and her pulse ran faster.

He was late.

Or was it possible that he wasn't coming?

She gnawed at her lip and moved away from the window, towards the table at the side of the meeting room. It had a selection of Danish pastries, a jug of fruit juice and bottles of cold water.

Skye opted for coffee, pouring a large measure into a fine bone-china cup and clasping it between her hands. It was reassuring to feel its warmth and smell its comforting aroma. Somehow, it grounded her.

A noise outside the door sounded and she froze, bracing herself for what was to come, knowing she would need all her wits about her to get through the next portion of her day.

The door pushed open and Charles Younger stood on the other side, incredibly handsome for a man in his sixties, with a kindly smile.

'Skye.' He nodded as he moved into the room.

But she wasn't looking at Charles.

Her eyes were greedy and they moved past the lawyer instantly, seeking the man she had been denied for so long. Matteo stepped into the room and everything froze. Time and physical existence.

It was all completely wrong. Being here with him yet not being able to touch him. Knowing she couldn't smile at him, even when she wanted so badly to pretend everything was as she'd thought—as she'd hoped.

Her own feelings overtook every other sense, but then, after only seconds, her eyes began to work properly, to see more than her own grief and heartache.

Her eyes saw him.

They saw the pallor of his skin and the grey beneath his eyes. The way his five o'clock shadow was more pronounced than ever, and the way his suit, which usually looked as though it had been lovingly stitched to his body, seemed loose and ill-fitting. She saw the way his eyes held hers for only a brief moment before moving away.

She saw in him something she recognised instantly, for it moved inside her.

She saw how he was broken.

And a sob filled her chest. She bit it back with effort, knowing she had to be strong.

'I'll be outside,' Charles said quietly. 'Just holler when you need me.'

Skye nodded curtly, a little more able to handle the situation given that she'd called the meeting and it was, more or less, on her home turf.

Charles left and silence fell. It sucked the air from the room and replaced it with something else altogether.

'Skye,' Matteo murmured, taking a step towards her and then pausing, his expression shifting. 'How are you?'

The question was her undoing, because he'd asked it in a way that had gone beyond civility. He asked as though knowing how she was meant everything to him.

'I'm...' She frowned. How could she respond? He looked as though he hadn't slept in weeks. Possibly hadn't eaten in that time either. 'Would you like something?' She grimaced as she heard the vague question leave her mouth. 'Croissant? Danish?'

His eyes glittered with a hint of the ruthlessness that was his stock in trade. She was glad to see it. She would take his ruthlessness over the sense of brokenness any day. 'Neither of those things.'

Her heart kerthunked.

'I'm glad you came,' she said softly, then cleared her throat and tried again. 'Please, take a seat.'

He arched a brow but did as she said, moving to one side of the table and sitting in a chair as though he owned it. That was an innate skill he possessed, she thought as she took the seat opposite. He commanded furniture, rooms, people, all effortlessly.

She cupped her coffee in front of herself and saw the moment his eyes dropped to her hands. Was he noticing that she didn't wear the wedding ring? Did he care?

Yes.

He cared. She couldn't deny that he was in pain, as she was.

The information felt strange inside her. Like a weight she didn't know how to carry.

'Well, Skye,' he drawled, his accent thick. 'Why am I here?'

She nodded, understanding that he wanted this over as quickly as she did. Pain lodged in her chest.

'I got your letter.'

'What letter?' he prompted, his brow furrowed.

'The hotel.' She didn't meet his eyes. 'The returned contracts.'

Silence prickled around the room. 'I sent that a long time ago.'

She shrugged. 'I just got it.' She thought of the

pile of mail she'd been stepping over and wondered when, exactly, the contracts had arrived. Charles had sent them almost as soon as she'd returned, with much disapproval and uncertainty about what Skye was proposing.

'I see.' He reclined back in his chair and she chanced a look at his face, then instantly wished she hadn't when her whole body seemed to catch fire. Her arms flecked with goose-bumps and desire slammed through her.

'I want you to have the hotel.' She leaned forward. 'It deserves to be what it used to be.'

His eyes narrowed. 'Then you are certainly able to renovate it.'

She recoiled as if he'd slapped her. How could she? How could she walk into the place that was like a living testament to Matteo? How could she oversee its renovations knowing that every colour scheme she chose or fitting she selected would be like touching Matteo all over again?

'No.' A terse word full of fear and meaning. 'I don't want it.'

'Nor do I,' he said softly. 'Unless you are part of the deal.'

'No more deals,' she whispered. 'Just common sense.'

'Common sense?' He arched a brow and then stood, moving towards the window. Skye's eyes captured every detail of him, greedily devouring him under the cover of his back being turned. She saw that he was, indeed, slimmer than he had been. That his hair was longer. That he was altered physically by what they'd experienced.

And guilt waved through her. Losing the baby had been a nightmare for her. But what about Matteo? She couldn't deny that he'd wanted their child. She didn't doubt that for a moment.

'How are you?' She whispered the question, the words full of haunted agony.

'How am I?' He spun around, pinning her with eyes that were full of Matteo, yet were not. Eyes that glowed with arrogance and pain. Eyes that were miserable.

'How am I?' he repeated, moving across the room towards her so that she held her breath and felt like she was being whipped with every step he took. His proximity was danger and delight.

'I am ruined, Skye.'

She couldn't hold her sob this time. It burst out of her but she said nothing. She could only stare and *feel*. Feel *everything*, all at once. All her hopes and loves and needs and wants, all her soul and her body and her heart.

'I am ruined.' He crouched before her and stared at her without touching. 'I am a half-man since you left. I have spent these weeks needing you, needing to hear your voice, to know that you are okay. Worrying for you, wishing for you. I have lived and breathed every day full of anger at my own stupidity. And the worst part of it is that you're right. You were right to walk out on me. After what I did to you, how can I hope you would love me still? You offered me your heart once and I was not man enough to understand what a gift it was. A stupid hotel! For a stupid hotel, I gambled you.'

Skye stared at him, her skin pricking with goose-bumps.

'I spent my life wanting that damned building, to the point I was blind to the truth of what we had. I hated your father, and I thought I was getting some petty kind of revenge in marrying you. And yet he has the last laugh, because I ruined even this. I fell in love with you and seem to have done everything I could to push you away.'

He dragged a hand through his hair. 'I have tormented myself with memories of all that I have said to you. Done to you. Of the way I have made it seem as though it's only your body I value, because I was too proud to admit how utterly you have all of me. How I rejected your love even when it was all I wanted.'

Skye bit back another sob, the grief of their situation permeating her body.

'I don't deserve you. I know that. But, even now, I need to know that you understand. That this is your decision. If you want me, I am yours.

I don't expect you to be stupid enough to give me another chance, Skye, but if you were... If you did...'

'Don't!' she cried, squeezing her eyes shut. 'This is hard enough...'

He reached for her hand and pressed it to his chest, and then he held his other palm flat against hers. 'Feel how we beat in unison. How our hearts know what we are too stupid to comprehend.'

She shook her head, tears stinging her eyes. 'Teo...'

He moved his hand from her chest and reached into the breast pocket of his suit. He pulled out a small velvet box and Skye froze, staring at her husband and then the little cube.

Before she could say anything, he popped the lid open and Skye's gaze fell to the ring.

And her chest rolled.

It was perfect.

Of their own volition, her fingertips moved to the ring and lifted it, staring at the details with a sense of awe. It was rose-gold with intricate patterns carved into the narrow band, and there were small diamonds set the whole way around. They were not of huge value, nor size, but they were beautiful.

'It's...very nice,' she said softly, sliding it back into the box.

Matteo's smile was just a quick twist of his

lips. 'It is what I should have chosen the first time around. I knew, as soon as you wore the other, that I had been wrong. That you are someone who prefers beauty over cost.'

She swallowed and looked away. 'The hotel...'

He shook his head, interrupting her with urgency. 'Do you remember what you said about love and hate? About how close they are on the emotional spectrum?'

Skye turned to face him, her eyes huge.

'I hated your father, Skye. I hated him practically my whole life, to an almost mythical proportion. I came here, to London, wanting the hotel more than anything in my life. I expected to hate you. I thought I could use you without experiencing even a hint of remorse over it.'

She hardened her heart and tilted her chin, telling herself to be strong even when she was grieving anew, like barely healed wounds were being sliced open.

'But I met you and everything changed. The world began to spin in entirely the wrong direction. Hate became love, but I didn't want to believe it. My idiocy makes it no less true, my darling, my love. Can you not see that I have loved you all along?'

Her expression was mutinous but hope flared large in her chest. 'You still tried to take the hotel.'

'Something I will always regret,' he murmured.

'Something I am trying to fix now, if you will let me. I want it out of our lives. It meant everything to me because it was such a big part of my family's history. But I will not jeopardise our future for my past.'

Skye swallowed, his words turning something around inside her. She remembered something else he'd said to her, what felt like a lifetime ago. *You are already smart. Why not be happy?*

'I don't know what to think. I don't know what to say. I feel one thing and I think another.'

'I know, I know.' He nodded gently, kneeling and pressing his forehead to hers. 'And you are right to question me. I *know* I will never hurt you again, but that it will take time to show you. So I ask you the same question I did in Venice on your last day. I know I have no right to even hope; that you have no reason to trust me. But, Skye, I ask only... Will you simply give me a chance to show you, *cara*?'

Her heart was trembling. 'I just... I don't think I can.' At his look of anguish, certainty filled her. 'The thing is, a chance isn't good enough.'

He nodded, putting some space between them.

'Then tell me what you need, *bella*. Tell me what will make you happy and I will do it.'

'Even if that means leaving? And never seeing me again?'

A muscle jerked in his cheek but he nodded.

'Yes, Skye.' She saw him swallow and brace himself, and she understood the emotions that were spreading through him. The pain and fear and miserable acceptance. But he continued bravely. 'I will never *not* love you. I will never not need you. But I will leave you alone…if this is what you want.'

And, finally, she smiled.

A smile that spread over her face and through her body. A smile that was definitely not matched by Matteo's expression.

'Why would I want you to leave me alone?'

He frowned, his confusion understandable.

'Oh, Matteo.' His name quivered against her mouth. 'I wish everything between us had been different.' She chewed on her lower lip thoughtfully. 'I wish there was no family feud, no hotel. No anger and hatred. But, even with things the way they were, I still loved you.'

His lips were grim. 'Because you are all that is kind and good. Only you could love a man like me…'

She held a hand up to silence him, pressing her fingertip to his lips. 'I married you because I loved you. I left you because I loved you too much to live with you, when you didn't feel the same way about me.'

'Only I did, *cara*. I've been such a damned fool.'

'Yes,' Skye murmured, narrowing her eyes thoughtfully. 'But, seeing as you've seen the light and are prepared to spend the rest of your life showing me each and every day just how much I mean to you, it would be rather foolish for me to make either of us suffer a moment longer. Right?' She lifted a hand to his cheek. 'We *are* both miserable, aren't we?'

His eyes swept over her face and he nodded, a grim gesture of agreement.

'So let's not be.' She lifted her hands and held his face, then moved her own closer.

'What exactly do you mean?' He was cautious, his expression guarded.

'You're my husband,' she said with an impish grin, mirroring a phrase he used often. She leaned her face forward, so their lips were only an inch apart. 'And I love you. As much now…no, more… than the day we married.'

His groan was heavy with emotion; his eyes swept shut. When he opened them again, Skye was staring at him, a smile on her sweet, pink lips.

'Do not kiss me,' he warned throatily. 'Or I will ravage you here and now.'

Skye's eyes twinkled. 'Then how about we go back to my place?'

'Right now?'

'Right now.'

* * *

They didn't make it upstairs.

They barely made it to her sofa. Skye welcomed her husband back into her home and her arms, needing to feel him more than she'd ever felt anyone or anything. He kissed her, he held her and he made love to her in a way that showed her what he'd been showing her all along.

There was no way their chemistry was just a physical thing.

It was all of them. It was everything.

She lay on his chest afterwards, her head pressed to his toned body, listening to the strong beating of his heart and knowing he was right— that it did indeed beat in unison with hers.

'Well, *cara*, what do you say?' he murmured against her hair, adjusting himself slightly as he reached to their pile of rumpled clothes on the floor beside them.

'About what?' The words were heavy with satisfaction and completion. She was energised and exhausted all at once.

He brought his hand close to her face and she blinked her eyes towards him, moving so that she could see him more clearly. She stared at the ring box, and her heart kerthunked against her ribcage.

'Would you consider wearing this ring? Will you be my wife?'

She wrinkled her nose. 'I *am* your wife.'

'Yes, you are,' he agreed, pulling the ring from its position and holding it towards her. Skye pushed up higher and held out her hand. Her fingertips were quivering.

'But I want the world to know it.' His eyes glittered with her possessively. 'With this ring, in this moment, with all my heart…' the words were gravelled '… I thee wed.'

She stared down at it and smiled, meeting his eyes and nodding. She wasn't even sure he'd asked a question, but she knew she needed to reassure him. To promise him that she had meant what she'd said in her lawyer's office.

'I had it inscribed,' he said huskily, holding the ring out to her.

She took it and lifted it closer to her eyes, peering into the fine gold band and reading the elegant scrawl.

Tu sei il mio sangue.

'You are my *sangue*?' she asked, repeating the final word aloud.

'You are my blood,' he said with a nod. 'And everything else of me. Always.'

A shiver of delight ran down her spine and she handed the ring back to him then extended her hand.

She watched as her husband slid the ring onto her finger—it fitted exactly. As though it had been designed for her.

'It's perfect.'

'As are you.' He pushed up and kissed her with a drugging, sensual need. 'It is very old. One of six that were made in the middle ages by a famous Venetian designer.'

She nodded, but she was moving over him already, her hands and her wedding ring tangling in his thick hair. Over his shoulder, her eyes caught sight of the gladioli she'd purchased over a week earlier. They had begun to bloom without her noticing and they stood now, proud and confident, filled with colour and light, the promise of all that they were fulfilled.

'You are as much a part of Venetian history as I am,' he murmured and she nodded, tears sparkling in her eyes.

'And I always will be.'

EPILOGUE

Two years later

'ARE YOU READY?' Skye asked her husband, smiling at him. She had expected to be nervous, given what they were about to do. But it was Matteo who showed all the signs of being on the brink of a breakdown.

Well, that was only fair.

This baby belonged to both of them, after all. They'd both helped make it, over long, exhausting months.

And now it was time.

Finally.

To show the world what the Vin Santos had achieved, side by side.

'As I'll ever be.' He squeezed her hand and his eyes roamed her face. *'Ti amo.'*

'Lo so.'

'Let's go.' The door to the car was opened and Matteo stepped out, standing aside to make room for his wife.

She was resplendent in a black ballgown. Cameras flashed everywhere, perfectly catching the bright red of the geraniums that tumbled in the moonlight from every window of the hotel.

'Have you heard news of the twins?' he asked, tucking a hand into the small of her back.

Skye's gaze drifted up past the brass flagpoles towards the perfectly restored windows that overlooked the river Tiber.

'The nanny texted just before. They have been asleep for over an hour.' She nodded. 'They're waiting for us in the penthouse.'

'Ah! I thought Francesca was going to give us some difficulties there,' he said.

'She never does travel well,' Skye agreed. 'Then again, she's only twelve months old. That's normal for this age, I believe.'

'And she is very cute.' He winked. 'Like her mother.'

Skye felt colour flush along to the roots of her hair, amazed at how his compliments could still turn her insides to mush.

'And Alfonso is just like you.'

'Yes.' Matteo grimaced. 'I'm sorry about that. His determination is a force to be reckoned with.'

Skye nodded. 'But we'll reckon with it together.'

The crowds parted to allow them entry into the hotel. Christmas Eve at Il Grande Fortuna for the first time in decades was just as magical as

Skye had hoped—it was everything she'd imagined from Matteo's stories and the photographs she'd seen. It was sublime.

'Shall we dance?'

Skye nodded, catching the classical Christmas carols and smiling. *'Si.'*

She put her hand in his and he held her tight, and with his body he promised everything she already knew to be true.

She was safe with him and she was loved by him.

They were a family.

And she'd never feel loneliness again.

* * * * *

If you enjoyed
Bound By The Billionaire's Vows
you're sure to enjoy these other stories
by Clare Connelly!

Her Wedding Night Surrender
Innocent In The Billionaire's Bed
Bought For The Billionaire's Revenge

Available now!